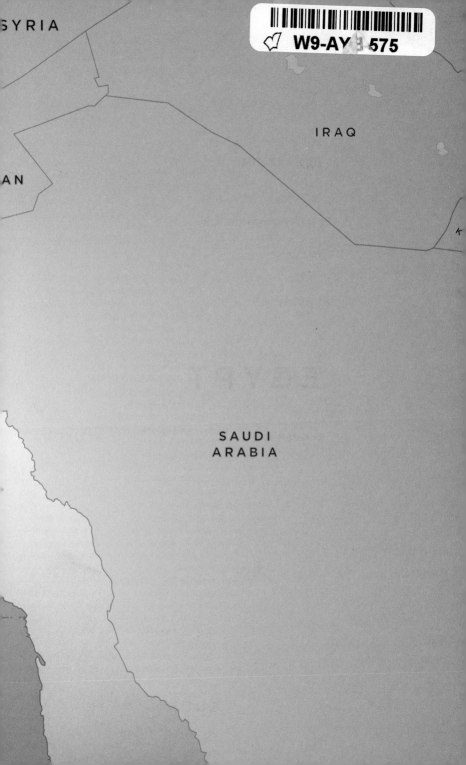

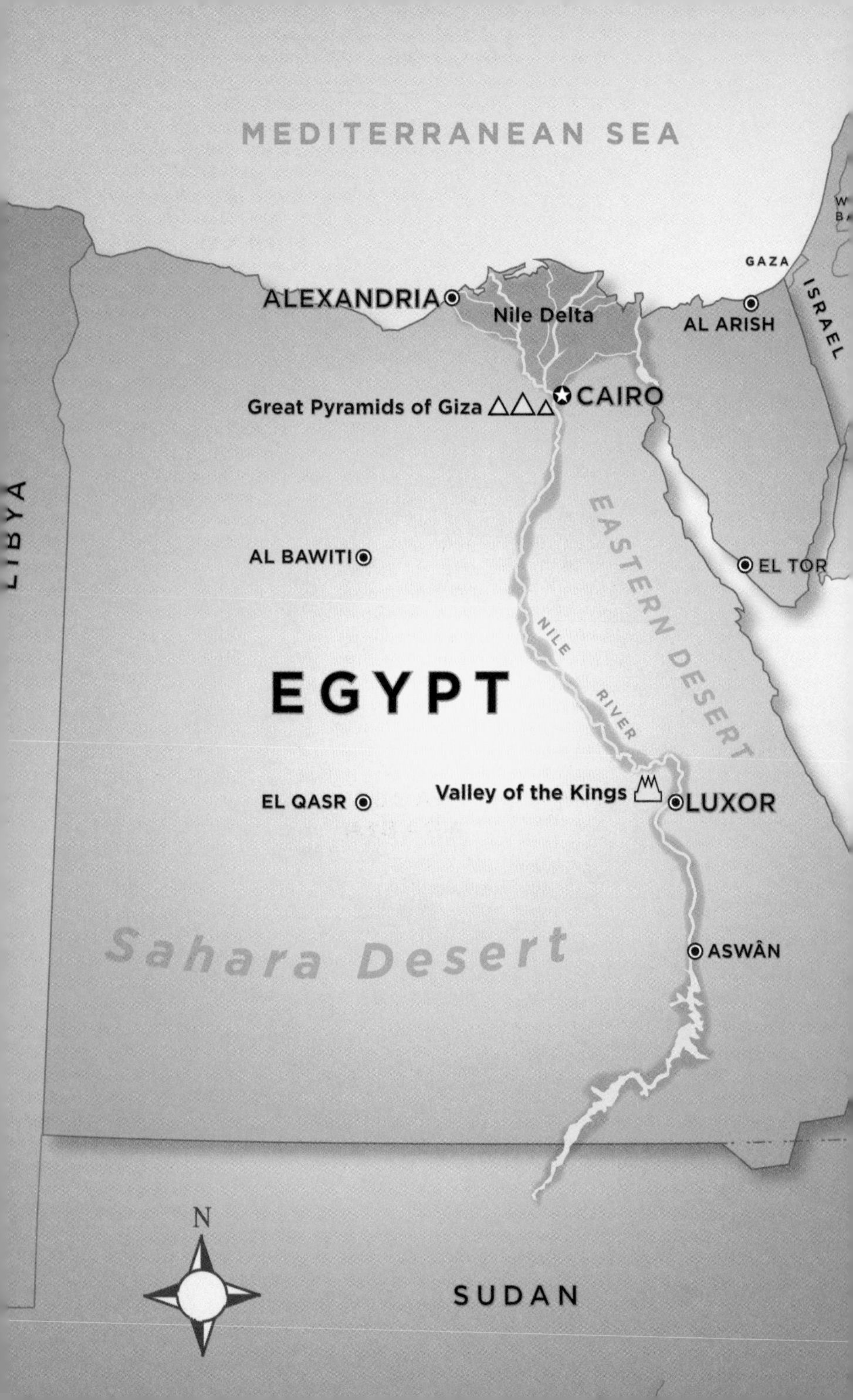

MEDITERRANEAN SEA

W
B

GAZA

LIBYA

ALEXANDRIA ◉

Nile Delta

AL ARISH

ISRAEL

Great Pyramids of Giza △△△ ★ CAIRO

AL BAWITI ◉

◉ EL TOR

EGYPT

EASTERN DESERT

NILE

RIVER

EL QASR ◉

Valley of the Kings 🏔 ◉ LUXOR

Sahara Desert

◉ ASWÂN

N

SUDAN

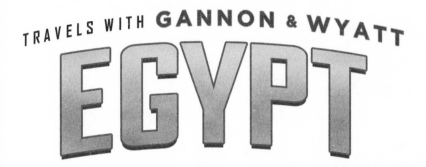

TRAVELS WITH GANNON & WYATT

EGYPT

PATTI WHEELER & KEITH HEMSTREET

GREENLEAF
BOOK GROUP PRESS

Published by Greenleaf Book Group Press
Austin, Texas
www.gbgpress.com

Distributed by Greenleaf Book Group LLC

For ordering information or special discounts for bulk purchases, please contact Greenleaf Book Group LLC at PO Box 91869, Austin, TX 78709, 512.891.6100.

Design and composition by Greenleaf Book Group LLC
Cover design by Leon Godwin & Greenleaf Book Group LLC
Cover illustration by Leon Godwin

Publisher's Cataloging-In-Publication Data

Wheeler, Patti.
  Travels with Gannon & Wyatt. Egypt / Patti Wheeler & Keith Hemstreet.—1st ed.
  p. : ill. ; cm.
  Summary: After winning a prestigious fellowship, twin explorers Gannon and Wyatt set off on a journey to Egypt to study with a world-renowned archaeologist. On their quest to find the long lost tomb of the Pharaoh Cleopatra, Gannon and Wyatt find that they aren't the only ones interested in Cleopatra's secrets. Ruthless tomb robbers are hot on their heels, and the brothers must brave venomous snakes, deadly booby traps, and ancient curses as they find themselves on the verge of a magnificent discovery that could rewrite history.
  Issued also as an ebook.
  ISBN: 978-1-60832-561-0
  1. Twins—Juvenile fiction. 2. Cleopatra, Queen of Egypt, -30 B.C.—Juvenile fiction. 3. Grave robbing—Egypt—Juvenile fiction. 4. Tombs—Egypt—Juvenile fiction. 5. Adventure and adventurers—Egypt—Juvenile fiction. 6. Egypt—Juvenile fiction. 7. Twins—Fiction. 8. Grave robbing—Egypt—Fiction. 9. Tombs—Egypt—Fiction. 10. Adventure and adventurers—Egypt—Fiction. 11. Egypt—Fiction. 12. Adventure stories. 13. Diary fiction. I. Hemstreet, Keith. II. Title. III. Title: Travels with Gannon and Wyatt. Egypt IV. Title: Egypt
  PZ7.W5663 Egy 2014
  [Fic]   2013946133

Part of the Tree Neutral® program, which offsets the number of trees consumed in the production and printing of this book by taking proactive steps, such as planting trees in direct proportion to the number of trees used: www.treeneutral.com.

Printed in the United States of America on acid-free paper

13 14 15 16 17 18   10 9 8 7 6 5 4 3 2 1

First Edition

TreeNeutral®

You can tell whether a man is clever by his answers.
You can tell whether a man is wise by his questions.

—Naguib Mahfouz, Egyptian winner
of the Nobel Prize in Literature

One hand doesn't clap.

—Egyptian Proverb

ENGLISH/ARABIC:
TRANSLATION OF COMMON PHRASES

Hello— As-salamu Alaykum

How are you?—Kayfa halluk

I am fine, thanks—Ana bkheir, shukran

What is your name?—Esmak Eh?

Please—Min fadhlik

Thank you—Shukran

No thank you—La Shukran

You're welcome—Afwan

Do you speak English?—Titkallam Inglizi?

I am lost—Ada'tu tareeqi!

Can you help me?—Hal beemkanek mosa'adati?

Can I help you?—Hal beemkani mosa'adatuk?

Okay—Tayib

Goodbye—Ma`a as-salaamah

CONTENTS

PART I

A LETTER FROM EGYPT

WYATT

Right up until this morning, you could say my career as an explorer was going exceptionally well. In all of our recent globe-trotting, my brother and I have saved endangered species, protected threatened habitats, and raised cultural awareness through the publication of our field notes.

I'm not going to lie, all of our success was starting to go to my head. I consider myself a humble guy. Honest, I do. But truth is, I've always pictured myself following in the footsteps of the great explorers—Captain James Cook, Dr. David Livingstone, Meriwether Lewis and William Clark. If you had asked me just this morning, I would have said with confidence that one day my name would be added to that list.

But, as they say, life is what happens while you're making other plans.

"It arrived, Wyatt!" I heard Gannon shout at the top of his lungs. "Hurry up and get down here so we can open it!"

I sprang from my desk chair, burst through the door of my bedroom and leapt down the stairs three at a time. Sprinting down the hall, I could see Gannon standing near the front door. In his hand was a large envelope. An envelope we'd been waiting almost three months to receive.

"Give it to me!" I said and snatched it away from him.

The envelope was scrawled with Arabic writing and covered in Egyptian postage. In the upper left corner was a faded black stamp that read:

```
Youth Exploration Society
   Cairo, Egypt Office
```

A few months back, Gannon and I applied for the Youth Exploration Society's Egyptian Antiquities Fellowship. Awarded annually to four lucky teenagers, this fellowship grants winners a one-month expedition in Egypt with a distinguished archeologist.

This year's fellowship is being led by none other than Dr. Mohammed Aziz, a man credited with discovering 99 tombs to date. It was my hope to be part of the team that helped him discover his 100th.

"Are you going to open it or just stare at it all day?" Gannon asked.

This was the moment of truth. At last, we were about to find out if we'd been chosen. I opened up the envelope and removed two letters.

"Read them aloud," Gannon said.

I cleared my throat.

```
Dear Gannon:
Congratulations! You are one of four candi-
dates that have been awarded the Egyptian
Antiquities Fellowship. Please keep this
```

```
between the two of us, but of all the can-
didates you were the most qualified. I look
very forward to having you on our team!

    Sincerely,
    Dr. Mohammed Aziz, Fellowship Director
    Youth Exploration Society
```

Gannon pumped his fist in the air.

"Oh, yeah!" he said. "I'm going to Egypt, baby!"

Something about the letter just didn't seem right. Gannon, the most qualified candidate? That's just ridiculous. The
second most qualified, maybe.

"Read your letter," Gannon said anxiously. "I'm dying to
know if you're going to Egypt with me."

I almost laughed at him.

"If they accepted you, they definitely accepted me."

I read the second letter.

```
Dear Wyatt:
Though we would like to accept you along
with your incredibly talented brother, the
competition this year was very stiff. I
regret to inform you that your application
has been denied. Better luck next year.

    Sincerely,
    Dr. Mohammed Aziz, Fellowship Director
    Youth Exploration Society
```

My ego deflated like an untied balloon. I was floored, shocked,
and worst of all, humiliated. Not only had I been denied, but
I'd lost out to my brother.

"Wow, that's a total bummer," Gannon said. " I was really hoping we'd be going to Egypt together. Oh, well."

How could this have happened? I still can't figure it out. There must have been some mistake. Maybe they mixed up our applications. Got our names crisscrossed. Given that we're twins, this seems a logical explanation. I bet they meant to accept me and deny Gannon. That's the only thing that makes any sense. After all, I'm the one who's been studying ancient Egypt for the past six months! I'm the one who loves archeology! I'm the aspiring scientist! As a fellow, I would make a meaningful contribution to the expedition! What's Gannon going to do in Egypt? Write poems about the desert?

I looked at my brother. He had a huge smile on his face.

"I can't believe this!" I yelled. "You don't even know anything about Egypt!"

"Don't be such a sore loser," he said. "I know plenty about Egypt."

"Okay, how tall is the Great Pyramid?"

"Much taller than you."

"455 feet."

"And how tall are you?" Gannon replied. "5′ 8″ tops? Next question."

"How many tombs have been discovered in the Valley of the Kings?"

"A lot."

"62, actually."

"Like I said, a lot. That's Gannon two, Wyatt zero. Just in case you're keeping score. Any more questions, smart guy?"

"Why don't you tell me something about Cleopatra?"

"*Cleopatra,* a 1963 film directed by Joseph L. Mankiewicz. The role of Cleopatra was played by Elizabeth Taylor."

"Are you being serious?"

"Come on, Wyatt. You should know better than to ask me movie trivia. I'm an aspiring filmmaker. You'll never stump me."

The discussion was pointless. My head sank.

"Keep your chin up, Wyatt," Gannon said. "You're no slouch of an explorer. I'd be willing to bet you came in fifth place. Not too shabby. It's like honorable mention. Who knows, maybe someone will drop out and you'll get to take their spot. I doubt it, but you never know."

Gannon patted me on the shoulder and walked off. I glared at him, my blood boiling, as he strolled down the hall whistling casually. If there's one thing Gannon's good at, it's rubbing salt in the wound. It makes losing to him almost unbearable. I had the urge to chase him down and give him a good pummeling, but I knew that wouldn't solve anything. Instead, I ran up to my room and haven't come out all afternoon.

Spread across my desk are several books on Egypt. *The Encyclopedia of Ancient Egypt* by Margaret Bunson; *Tutankhamen* by Howard Carter; *Cleopatra: A Life* by Stacy Schiff. There are drawings of tombs, diagrams of the tunnels and chambers in the Great Pyramid, maps of the Nile River, Cairo, Alexandria, and Luxor.

To think of the hours I've spent studying. All those late nights and weekends preparing an application that I thought was a sure thing. As far as I know, Gannon hasn't done anything to prepare. I guess none of that matters now. Bottom line, he's going to Egypt and I'm not.

GANNON
DECEMBER 14

Okay, okay, I should probably 'fess up. Let's see, how can I put this? I totally messed with my brother's head. Yeah, that's one way. I toyed with his emotions. Sure, that's another. I betrayed his trust in me. Fair enough, I guess that's another, but I like the first two better. They don't sound quite as harsh.

So what did I do to poor Wyatt?

Well, just so happens I was outside this morning when Easy Eddy, our mailman, drove up.

"Hey, Easy Eddy!" I said. "How's it going?"

"Takin' it easy," he said.

"Easy's the only way to take it."

"Right on, brother."

He handed me a stack of mail, shot me the "hang loose" sign, and drove off with his music blaring. I was flipping through the mail as I walked inside and that's when I saw the envelope from Egypt. Pretty much goes without saying that I had to be the first to know if either of us had won the fellowship, so I opened it right away.

When I read that we had both won, I was so excited and almost yelled to Wyatt, but just before I did I was hit with this brilliant idea and instead made a beeline to my dad's office. There, I hid the acceptance letter and typed up two fake letters. One that said I was accepted and another that said Wyatt had been denied. I slid the fake letters into the envelope and resealed it with tape. Oh, man. After Wyatt read those letters he went totally pale and his mouth fell wide open. I'm not joking, it looked like he'd just seen sasquatch or something.

So, do I regret doing such a jerky thing? Are you kidding? No way. Like I said, he's my twin. I would have regretted not doing it.

Of course, my mom wasn't so amused.

"How could you do that to your brother?" she yelled. "You know how much this fellowship means to him. Go apologize right now. Otherwise, I'll call Dr. Aziz and tell him that Wyatt will be coming to Egypt alone."

"Fine," I said. "I'll apologize."

If it were up to me, I'd totally let this joke ride another day. Probably two. But, I guess a few hours of torture is enough. Poor Wyatt's been locked in his room all afternoon, probably pouting over the thought of having to stay at home, farting around with his microscopes and Petri dishes, while I'm blazing trails in Egypt.

Oh, jeez. Too funny!

WYATT

When Gannon told me that he had actually written the letters as a joke and that we'd both really won the fellowship, I almost snapped. A practical joke that cruel deserves serious payback, but at the same time I was so happy that I was going to Egypt I hardly even cared.

I pushed him aside and yelled to my parents:

"Mom, Dad! We won the Youth Exploration Society fellowship! We're going to Egypt!"

My parents walked into the kitchen.

"I heard," my mom said, narrowing her eyes at Gannon.

"Congratulations, boys," my dad said. "That's quite an honor. When does the fellowship begin?"

"In February," Gannon said. "We'll be getting a call in a couple days with more details."

My mom was already thinking ahead.

"Let me know the dates," she said. "I'll call crew scheduling and see if I can work the New York–Cairo flight so we can all fly together."

My dad couldn't wait to set up an easel and canvas on a high dune above the Great Pyramids of Giza and make an oil painting. He's also a great sculptor and was anxious to study the sculpting techniques that the ancient Egyptians used to create some of their most famous monuments, like the Great Sphinx.

"I'm really excited to visit Egypt again," my mom said. She lived in Cairo for several months when she was in college as part of a study abroad program. While she was there she spent some time working at a learning center for children. "I'm going to call some friends and see about volunteering at a literacy program in the city. Did you know that nearly 30 percent of the Egyptian population can't read or write? That should serve as a reminder to you boys. Don't ever take your education for granted."

Even though our home-schooling routine can be a real pain sometimes, she did have a point. There's no denying it, my mom is an amazing teacher.

"Since we're on the topic of education," she continued, "you better put in some extra study time tonight. Your algebra mid-term is tomorrow."

Gannon's shoulders slumped.

"Thanks for the reminder, mom," he said. "Come on, Wyatt. I'll show you how to do all those problems you don't understand."

"Yeah, right," I said as we walked off towards our room. "I could do algebra in my sleep. And after that stunt you pulled with the acceptance letter, don't even think about asking me for help."

"Fair enough," Gannon said, laughing again at the joke he'd played on me. "Fair enough."

GANNON

Our flight from Colorado was bumpy right after take off, which isn't all that unusual when you fly out of Denver, but no matter how many times I go through it I still get all fidgety and sweaty and today was no different. After we got to a certain altitude, though, the plane steadied and I was able to kick back in my seat and relax the rest of the way across the country.

Aerial view of Midwestern U.S.

We arrived in New York's LaGuardia Airport sometime late afternoon with a few hours to burn before our next flight, so we ducked into an airport café and polished off some chicken strips and soggy fries, then went browsing around the duty-free shops. I bought a new inflatable neck pillow and some spearmint gum for the long flight and by then it was time to make our way to the gate.

I'm in seat 36B, a dreaded middle seat. Wyatt's also stuck in a middle seat several rows back. Of course, my dad lucked out. He's in an aisle seat, so, naturally, I tried to swindle him out of it.

"Here's what we'll do," I said. "I'll flip this quarter. Heads I win the aisle seat. Tails you lose it."

"I may have been born at night," my dad said, "but it wasn't last night."

So here I am, crammed between two Egyptian men who don't speak a lick of English. It seems my mom should get some kind of preferential seating, being a long-time flight attendant for the airline and all, but that's not how it works. We have to take whatever seats are available, which, I guess, is the only real downside of the airline's free flying policy for families. Not that I'm complaining.

The flight from New York City to Cairo is about eleven and a half hours. I'd say we've been airborne for about two hours now, give or take, but it seems more like ten. Wyatt told me Cairo time is six hours ahead of New York, so factoring in our flying time and the time zone changes and all that, we should be landing around 4:00 PM tomorrow . . . that is, if my calculations are correct, and that's never a given. I'll say this, whatever time we land, I definitely foresee a case of jetlag in my future.

Since we took off, I've had my English-Arabic dictionary spread across my lap and have been practicing some phrases. "As-salamu Alaykum," is the most common greeting in Arabic. People say it like English speakers say "hello," but it really means, "peace be upon you." Of course, "As-salamu Alaykum" is the phonetic spelling, which basically means that it's written using the English alphabet so that people like me can read it. Written in Arabic, "As-salamu Alaykum" looks like this:

السلام عليكم

Thank goodness for the phonetic spelling, because I'd have some trouble sounding that out.

My mom's always said that there's no better way to learn a new language than to talk with native speakers, so I tested out some phrases on the two men sitting next to me.

"As-salamu Alaykum," I said.

"As-salamu Alaykum," each responded.

I looked back to my dictionary, scanning the page for something else to say.

"Kef halak?" I finally asked, which means, "how are you?"

One of them said a bunch of stuff and I didn't know what

any of it meant, but still, I didn't want to seem rude by not responding, so I quickly reverted to English.

"Okay, great," I said.

"Great," the other man repeated.

I looked back to my book.

"Esmak Eh?" I asked, which in English means, "What is your name?"

"Mohammed," the man to my left said.

I turned to the other man and asked the same.

"Mohammed," he replied.

"Really?" I said. "You're both named Mohammed? What a coincidence."

"Mohammed," one of them repeated, nodding.

"My name is Gannon."

"Ganyon," one of the men said, like "Canyon," but with a "G."

"Gannon," I said again, slowly.

"Gah-noon," he said, making a second attempt.

"Close enough."

They both smiled.

I was really having fun talking with both Mohammeds, but to have a real conversation and actually learn something about these guys, like where they're from and what they do for a living and stuff like that, I'd need to know a heck of a lot more Arabic.

"Right, well, it's been nice talking to you," I said and pointed to my dictionary, "but I'm going to keep studying."

"Yes," Mohammed to my left said.

"Study," said Mohammed to my right.

I nodded and just like that, our conversation was over.

Okay, that's enough journaling for now. Hand's cramping. More later . . .

WYATT

FEBRUARY 22, 12:14 AM
NORTH OF BERMUDA
42,194 FEET OVER THE ATLANTIC OCEAN

There aren't many things I enjoy more than the start of a new adventure, all the build up as the day draws near, wondering what we might see and learn when we get there. And then, finally, the day comes. Well, today is one of those days. We're officially en route to Egypt, and this adventure holds big promise.

Long flights provide lots of quiet time for reading and writing. I've got my overhead light on and all my notes spread out on the plane's tray table along with a few books that I was able to stuff into my backpack.

Egypt was home to one of the world's great civilizations. It's really amazing what they were able to accomplish thousands of years ago. How they did it all is somewhat of a mystery. Fact is, scientists still don't know for sure how the Great Pyramids of Giza were actually built. And new discoveries are being made all the time. That's what has me really excited about this expedition. Important discoveries can still be made. Discoveries that could rewrite history!

Archeologically speaking, Egypt has a long list of incredible finds. There's the discovery of the Pharaoh Khufu's wooden ship within the Great Pyramid. It's around 4,600 years old and was built so well, scientists say it could still sail today. Then there's the discovery of the Valley of the Golden Mummies, which was found when a donkey's leg sunk into a hole. It's a huge burial ground and many of the mummies there are gilded, which means they're covered in a layer of gold. But the most famous discovery has to be the Tomb of Tutankhamen (also spelled Tutankhamun). This tomb was discovered by archeologist Howard Carter in 1922, and was full of incredible treasures, including a solid gold sarcophagus that held King Tut's mummified body.

Tomb of King Tut, who died at age 19

The goal of our fellowship is to add a discovery to the top of this list.

The discovery of Cleopatra!

During her reign, Cleopatra was the most powerful woman in the world. She was also the last Pharaoh of Egypt and is considered by many to be the most famous woman to ever live. For thousands of years, the final resting place of Cleopatra has been a mystery. There's no question about it, to find her would be an archeologist's dream come true!

All right, it's getting late. Most people on the plane are sleeping. Time to recline this seat a few inches and join them.

GANNON

Okay then . . . haven't slept a wink. As for Mohammed right and left, they'll definitely be well rested when we land. I mean, these guys have been sleeping like babies—big, scruffy, loudly snoring babies. I asked my mom for ear plugs, but they had already given them all away, so I tried rolling up little wads of tissue and stuffing them in my ears, but that didn't work so well. I guess tissue isn't very good at blocking sound. We should be landing in about an hour and it goes without saying, I'm counting the seconds.

Just a little while ago, Wyatt handed me a book and went back to his seat to get some sleep. Inside there was a dog-eared page and a note he'd written that said: "Gannon, must read!"

So I read.

If his goal was to make me nervous about our explorations in Egypt, he did a bang up job. According to this book, lots of people believe that anyone who disturbs an ancient tomb will be cursed. Okay, fine. Whatever. I kind of knew that already, but what I didn't know was how many stories there are to back this superstition. Take the discovery of King Tut's tomb, for example. Howard Carter, the archeologist who led the dig, had a canary at the site for good luck. Well, the day they discovered the steps to the tomb, a cobra snuck into the cage and killed the bird. Now, I don't know about Howard Carter, but if my good luck charm was eaten by a snake, I'd probably take that as a bad sign.

Sure enough, not long after, tragedy struck.

The dig was paid for by an Englishman named Lord Carnarvan. Without his money, Howard Carter wouldn't have been able to pay all the workers to do the excavating, so I suppose it could be said that Lord Carnarvan was the man responsible for the dig. Well, the canary incident didn't scare Howard Carter or Lord Carnarvan. They weren't going to stop digging for anything and kept right on until they found King Tut's burial chamber. Five months later, Lord Carnarvan died, "mysteriously."

Here's the thing: I don't care to die mysteriously, or by any explainable means either. I still have lots of living to do. Lots of things to see and people to meet and places to go.

Call me selfish, but there are few things more important to me than *me*.

Now, I'm sure all this stuff would sound totally ridiculous to someone who doesn't believe in superstitions, but unfortunately I'm a superstitious kind of guy and in my mind an ancient curse is just the sort of thing that could bring this fellowship to a disastrous end.

Let's hope I'm wrong.

WYATT

FEBRUARY 22, 3:56 PM EET (EASTERN EUROPEAN TIME)
CAIRO INTERNATIONAL AIRPORT
20° CELSIUS, 68° FAHRENHEIT

The first thing I noticed as I stepped off the plane in Cairo were the men with guns. Four soldiers in black fatigues walked along the beltway. Each was holding a submachine gun. Another group of security officers dressed in white uniforms and armed with pistols on their hips ushered passengers towards immigration and customs.

"As-salamu Alaykum," Gannon said to one of the men as we passed. "Cool gun," he said to another.

Neither man responded.

"Stop talking, Gannon," I said. "Can't you see that they don't want you bothering them?"

"I'm just trying to be friendly."

"What you call friendly they probably call annoying."

My dad, Gannon, and I boarded the tram that would take us to the border patrol. My mom had to finish up her post-flight duties and planned to meet us at the hotel.

"So, boys," my dad said, "how are you feeling after that nice, long flight?"

"Surprisingly, not so bad," Gannon said.

"I feel pretty good, too," I said.

No matter how far away, I always feel good when I arrive in a new destination. The adrenaline just starts flowing. It's that first introduction to a different landscape, language, or culture. It gives me a little boost. There's so much to take in that it overcomes any exhaustion I feel from the long flight.

Exiting the tram, we were led by more guards to baggage claim and then directed to a line where we waited to pass through immigration and customs. When it came our turn, the agents were very thorough. Our equipment was inspected multiple times, and our clothes were rummaged through, wadded into balls, and tossed haphazardly back into our bags.

"Don't worry about refolding anything," Gannon said, sarcastically. "I'll do it later."

They simply ignored him, stamped our passports and waved us through.

Dr. Aziz was waiting in the airport lobby to greet us. A stocky man, with graying hair and a friendly face, Dr. Aziz is known for his charming personality. Wherever he goes, he's the center of attention. He must have recognized us from our application photos, because as soon as we came across the lobby he jumped from his chair.

"Gannon and Wyatt!" he shouted happily.

We made our way to him and shook hands.

"Well, well, well," he continued. "If it isn't the talented twin explorers, in the flesh."

Caught off guard by his enthusiastic welcome, all we could think to do was laugh.

"Dr. Mohammed Aziz, at your service," he said and bowed humbly. "Welcome to Egypt, my friends!"

His energy was contagious.

"It's a pleasure to be here," I said. "I can't tell you how excited we are to be a part of this archeological expedition."

Standing behind Dr. Aziz were a boy and a girl, both about our age.

"I would like you to meet the other fellowship winners," Dr. Aziz said. "This is James, all the way from Alice Springs, Australia. His work to date has focused on the history of the Aborigines. He has personally found human artifacts in the Lake Mungo area of Australia that date back 40,000 years!"

"It's the land where time began," James said. "How do you do, mates? It's great to meet you."

"Likewise," I said, shaking his hand.

"And this lovely lady is Serene," Dr. Aziz said. "A promising young archeologist born and raised right here in Cairo. She was part of the crew that helped discover the Valley of the Golden Mummies."

"I read all about it," I said. "What an amazing discovery."

"Thank you," Serene said. "I've been fortunate enough to work with some of Egypt's greatest archeologists. The credit, or course, belongs to them."

"Is it Serene, as in the word meaning calm and peaceful?" Gannon asked.

"That's right," she said.

"What a beautiful name."

She had long dark hair, olive skin, and emerald-colored eyes that were so unique they demanded your attention. She wore blue jeans, a coat, and a loose-fitting scarf around her neck.

"What does Gannon mean?" she asked.

"It's Gaelic," Gannon said. "It means fair-haired one."

"Fits you perfect, mate!" James said with a laugh.

"Yeah, I guess it does."

"May we all have success on our expedition," Dr. Aziz said. "In the end, I hope you will have had a wonderful experience in our country."

"Doctor," my dad said, patting Gannon on the shoulder, "this one's a little superstitious. He's afraid you might all get cursed."

"Come on, Dad?" Gannon said, embarrassed. "Did you really have to bring that up?"

My dad laughed. Like me, he doesn't give much merit to superstitions and likes to tease Gannon, who, of course, buys into them wholeheartedly.

"You need not worry about ancient curses," Dr. Aziz said. "Do you know why?"

"Why?" Gannon asked.

"Because as an archeologist, there is nothing you can do to protect yourself against them. It is true, many archeologists have experienced tragic ends. Were they cursed? Maybe. Some certainly believe so, but scientifically speaking, there is no way to prove it. Coping with your superstitions is simply part of the job."

"Feel better, Gannon?" my dad asked.

"Oh, sure," Gannon said. "Much better."

Dr. Aziz laughed.

"This I promise," he said. "The adventure that lies before you will be the thrill of a lifetime. Very few people your age get the opportunity to see the places you are going to see. And if we have success, our findings might very well land all of your names in the history books!"

GANNON

NILE HOTEL
7TH FLOOR, ROOM #721

Okay, we just arrived this afternoon, but my head is already spinning with the sights and sounds of Cairo so before I hit the sack I need to write down some of my initial thoughts on the city, and I have a few.

First of all, it's big. Like, bursting-at-the-seams big.

According to Wyatt, at the last census there were 17 million people in the greater Cairo metropolitan area, making it the biggest city in Africa and one of the most densely populated cities on the planet. So, goes without saying, this city is swarming with people—hordes making their way along busy sidewalks, masses mingling in the square, crowds on every street corner—basically, people everywhere!

Bustling downtown Cairo

Second, Cairo is a city where old and new exist side by side. Literally, ancient mosques dating back thousands of years stand right alongside modern skyscrapers. There are groups of women in traditional black robes walking next to women dressed in the latest fashions. Scattered here and there among the traffic are donkey-drawn carts toting all kinds of stuff—caged chickens and pigeons, piles of fruit and vegetables, or in some cases, entire families. I also saw some goat herders moving through the pedestrians downtown as casually as if they were on a farm. And speaking of farms, I saw one of those too, a shanty kind of thing built in an alleyway next to a car dealership with a makeshift fence holding a dozen or so sheep and a boney cow.

Third, traffic is, well, how should I put this? Okay, it stinks. I'm not kidding, the exhaust from all of the cars is so thick at times it made me feel like I was going to vomit. And judging by the way people drive, I don't think there are traffic laws in Cairo. I mean, if there are, people totally ignore them. Drivers here make their own rules and communicate with their horns. As far as I could tell, there's a code. One honk means, "move it." Two honks means, "Seriously, move it." Three honks means, "I'm getting impatient, so, please, move it for real!" Finally, one long, hard blast of the horn means, "I'm very aggravated that you are ignoring me and if you don't move it right this second we are going to have a problem, you and I!"

I can't imagine getting my driver's license in a city like Cairo. For real, I don't think I'd pass the driver's test. Then again, maybe you don't even need a license here. Maybe they just let anyone get behind the wheel and that's part of the problem.

Cairo traffic

Oh, and here's something I've never seen before: The crosswalk signs don't show a "walker" when it's safe to cross. They show a "runner." No joke. There's a little guy made of white lights that runs when it's time to cross, because if people don't run, they'll get run over.

By the time we reached the hotel, I felt totally nauseous and staggered out of the car and took a bunch of long, deep breaths. The air outside the hotel wasn't much better than the exhaust-filled taxi, but it definitely felt good to be on stable ground.

"Esmak Eh?" I asked the cab driver.

"Mohammed," he answered.

"You've got to be kidding me," I said. "I've met four

Egyptian men today and every one of them has been named Mohammed."

"You're in Egypt," he said. "Almost all men are named Mohammed."

"Oh, you speak English?"

"Yes, I do."

"Well, Mohammed. I'm going to be honest, I thought I might throw up in the back of your cab during that wild ride, but I will say this, you're one of the best drivers I've ever met. How you got us to the hotel without getting in ten accidents is nothing short of a miracle."

"As you say in America," he said, "piece of cake."

We gathered all of our stuff, shook Mohammed's hand, and checked in. We're staying at The Nile Hotel for a couple nights. It's on the banks of the river right across the street from the Cairo Zoo. From the balcony of our room, I can see a bunch of hippos swimming around in a pond. No joke. I even heard a lion roar, which is a totally crazy thing to hear in a city like this. Anyway, from Cairo, we'll be going south to the town of Luxor and the Valley of the Kings for archeological training. Then we'll make our way to an excavation site in the desert somewhere near Alexandria where we will join the search for Cleopatra.

I didn't sleep at all on the plane to Egypt and I've got that weird long-flight, numb-body, foggy-headed thing going on. To tell the truth, I'm about to fall flat on my face, so, yeah, time for bed.

Goodnight, Cairo . . . .

WYATT

We woke this morning before sunrise to the sound of the Islamic Call to Prayer. Five times a day, the call to prayer, or adhan, is broadcast from loud speakers throughout the Arab world. The broadcast calls Muslims to pray, giving thanks for all of life's blessings. I stepped onto our balcony to listen to this melody. It was almost hypnotic as it echoed through the city streets. To the east, the sun was coming up on the horizon. Below us, the Nile River flowed, a tranquil, slow-moving waterway in an otherwise bustling city.

Since the fellowship doesn't officially begin until tomorrow, Gannon and I decided to check out the Khan al-Khalili Bazaar, one of the oldest markets in the world. They sell just about everything you can imagine here; from spices to pottery, jewelry to belly dancing costumes, perfume to replica artifacts. In almost every shop you can find an impressive collection of tiny pyramids, sphinx statues, and mini-sarcophaguses. Without question, the most popular gift is anything that has to do with King Tut. There are pencils, pens, posters, plates, T-shirts, baby toys, and just about anything else you can stamp the young King's face on.

These shopkeepers here have a real knack for display.

Golden sculptures for sale at the bazaar

Everything is lined neatly on shelves, organized by size, stacked at varying heights, and polished to give the appearance of a Pharaoh's treasure. And there is always a man dusting the merchandise.

The shopkeepers are also expert salesmen. There is no such thing as peaceful browsing at the Khan al-Khalili Bazaar. It's rare to pass a shopkeeper that doesn't try to lure us into his store with questions and conversation.

"Hey, boys!" they'll shout. "Where are you from? Ah, Americans! What a coincidence! I am American, too! You stick with me. I have everything you need at the best price!"

Others are more straightforward.

"Hello, boys," they'll say as we pass. "How can I take your money?"

Our cab driver, a young college student studying at Cairo University, gave us some advice before we wandered into the bazaar.

"You will not see any price tags on the merchandise," he said. "That's because there are no set prices. Khan al-Khalili is a hagglers' market. To haggle means to negotiate the price. Have you ever haggled?"

"Not really," Gannon said.

"Then be careful. The first price vendors will give you is the tourist price. That's the price you do not want to pay. Try to haggle with them and get a lower price. And don't be afraid to walk away if you think they are trying to rip you off. In the end, they want your business and will settle for a price you're comfortable with."

I wasn't looking for anything in particular, but wound up buying an Egyptian soccer jersey for myself. Gannon and I also found a sterling silver jewelry box for our three-year-old cousin, Emerson. She's young, but already loves jewelry.

"How much?" Gannon asked, pointing to the silver box.

"500 Egyptian pounds," the man replied.

"No way," Gannon protested. "That price is higher than a camel's butt. Come on, my friend. Work with me here."

Despite Gannon's attempt at haggling, we still ended up paying the tourist price.

Exhausted after walking many miles, Gannon and I took a seat at a café under a colorful umbrella and ordered some iced tea and a basket of falafels. A traditional Middle-Eastern dish, falafels are mashed chickpeas pressed into a patty, mixed with all sorts of spices, and deep-fried. They're typically served with flatbread and hot sauce.

"Very popular street food," our waiter said in broken English. "Make you strong man!"

"Good," I said. "Gannon needs some help in that department."

"Ha-ha," Gannon quipped.

We devoured our first basket within minutes, ordered another, and stuffed it down just as quick. We're so full right now we can hardly move. I'm enjoying this time, just relaxing under the shade of an umbrella and writing in my journal as this bustling bazaar happens all around us, but we should probably get back to the hotel soon. We've got a big day tomorrow.

GANNON
BACK AT HOTEL
NIGHT

Important matters such as souvenir hunting cannot be rushed. Patience is key. For real, it's the difference between finding something you cherish for the rest of your life and settling for something that ends up in the back of your closet, covered in dust, forgotten and unappreciated.

Unfortunately, patience is a virtue my brother totally lacks. I mean, we'd only been at the bazaar for a few hours and he was ready to pack it in and head back to the hotel.

"Let's get a cab," he said, after we finished lunch.

"Not yet," I said, "I still need to get something for myself."

"We just walked down every street in the bazaar. Why didn't you get something then?"

"I didn't come across the right souvenir, that's why. When you visit a place like Egypt, you have to leave with something special. A pyramid paperweight won't do. It has to be a souvenir that has meaning."

"Fine," Wyatt said, "But you better find this meaningful thing pronto or I'm heading back to the hotel without you."

So, we headed back into the bazaar. After some meandering, I spotted a store that looked interesting.

The crowds at Khan al-Khalili

"Look," I said, pointing down an alleyway. "We haven't been in this place. Let's check it out."

At the end of the alley there was this doorway with brass lanterns hanging on both sides and white lights strung around the door-frame. We stepped through the door into a small, narrow shop. The place was lit with dozens of candles all melted down into blobs and there were three rows of shelving on either wall and each was stacked with all kinds of little trinkets that flickered in the candlelight. Seated in the corner was an old man, puffing away on a long wooden pipe.

"Titkallam Inglizi?" I asked. This was another important phrase I'd learned. It means, "Do you speak English?"

The man nodded.

"What kind of store is this?" I asked.

"That depends," he said. "What are you looking for?"

"Here we go again," Wyatt said under his breath.

For whatever reason, I had a good feeling about this guy. Maybe it was that he didn't immediately come off as pushy like a lot of the other vendors we'd come across.

"I'm looking for something that's one of a kind," I said.

"Let me ask you a question," the shopkeeper said. "What is it that brings you to Egypt?"

"We're on an archeological expedition," I answered.

"What are you searching for?" he asked.

"Cleopatra."

The man looked at us curiously.

"Searching for the Queen," he finally said. "That is very ambitious of you."

I nodded in agreement.

"You are aware that Cleopatra's whereabouts have eluded some of the world's greatest archeologists?" he asked.

"Yes, we're aware," I said, looking at an old record player he had on his shelf. "Wow, this is pretty cool."

Wyatt immediately protested, whispering into my ear.

"You're not buying a record player, Gannon."

"Calm down," I whispered back. "I just said it was cool, that's all."

The man had stopped smoking, but he kept staring at us.

"Since we're on the topic of Cleopatra," I said to him, "do you have anything that dates back to the time of her reign?"

"I was hoping you'd ask," he said with a mischievous grin. "Follow me."

I raised my eyebrows to Wyatt as the shopkeeper disappeared behind a curtain in the back corner of the store.

"Come on, Gannon. Don't be stupid. This guy's going to scam you."

"Let's just see what he wants to show us. It's not like I have to buy it."

"I know you. You're a total sucker. I'd be willing to bet he ends up with every last Egyptian pound in your wallet."

We followed the man through a storage area that exited into an alley so narrow that we had to turn sideways to squeeze through it.

Wyatt was getting really nervous.

"This isn't smart," he whispered.

"Relax, bro," I said.

"You know what Mom and Dad would do if they knew we were following a complete stranger down some creepy alleyway?"

"This is just the kind of experience that leads to the best souvenirs."

"Or a kidnapping."

A short way into the alley it opened up and we came to a small courtyard closed off on all sides by high buildings.

"Just up this ladder," the shopkeeper said.

"I'm not going," Wyatt said, quietly.

"This guy's harmless," I said under my breath. "Look at him."

We both turned to the man and he smiled, showing off his teeth, which were all crooked and brown with a few missing here and there. Okay, it might not have been a pretty smile, but it was sincere.

"See?" I said.

Wyatt took a deep breath.

"Fine, but if this turns out bad, I'm telling Mom and Dad it was all your idea."

"Whatever."

"After you," the shopkeeper said.

Looking up the rusty ladder that led to an even rustier balcony, I had second thoughts myself.

"You sure about this?" I asked the shopkeeper.

"It is safe," he said. "I promise. You will not be disappointed."

"You know what," I said. "I'll follow you."

So, up he went. I followed. Wyatt was close behind.

At the top of the ladder, we climbed through a window into a small room where all kinds of dust was swirling through the air. Everything inside was covered in bed sheets that had turned yellow with age.

"What's all this?" I asked right before I sneezed.

"These are my treasures," the man said, and carefully drew back a sheet. Underneath was a shelf full of random artifacts. He reached up and took in his hand what looked like a broken piece of pottery.

"My grandfather was an archeologist," he continued. "His name was Rifa'a Kamil. He made many great discoveries and was well respected by his peers. The one thing that always escaped him was the tomb of Cleopatra."

Now this guy really had my attention.

"At the end of his life my grandfather was confident he was close to finding the Queen's final resting place. He was rather secretive about his work. No one knew the exact location of the dig, but I do know he was in the northern deserts not far from Alexandria. He was afraid if he gave the exact coordinates, others would show up and rob the tomb. This broken tile is the only relic he ever brought back. See the profile carved into the stone?"

"It looks like a woman."

"It is a woman," the shopkeeper said. "Cleopatra."

My eyes almost popped out of my head.

Wyatt scoffed.

"What ever happened to your grandfather's excavation?" I asked.

"One winter, he returned to the site of the dig saying that he would be home in the spring. While he was there, a major sandstorm settled over Alexandria. It lasted for weeks. We never saw him again."

"He disappeared?"

"Most likely buried where he stood."

Wyatt leaned over and whispered in my ear.

"This guy is full of it," he said. "What are the chances that this piece is actually from Cleopatra's tomb? I'll tell you. Slim to none. I bet he broke a tile in his shop and now he's trying to cover his losses by selling it to you. Don't be an idiot."

"How much?" I asked the shopkeeper.

"If you buy it I'm disowning you as a brother," Wyatt said.

The shopkeeper ran his dry, calloused fingers over the piece.

"The artifacts in this room have never been for sale," he said. "However, I am an old man now. Since my days remaining on this earth are numbered, I've decided that certain pieces should be given to the right people. My instinct tells me you are the right person."

"Did you say given?" I asked. "As in for free?"

The man nodded.

"Thank you, sir!" I said excitedly.

"First, you must make me a promise. This is not a souvenir. I believe in my heart that it is truly a piece from Cleopatra's tomb, which makes it an archeological treasure whose value is beyond measure. You must respect it as such."

"I promise to honor your wishes."

Apparently he felt my promise was genuine and that he could trust me. He carefully handed me the piece. I'm not lying, as soon as my fingertips touched it this crazy tingling sensation ran all the way up my arm and into my shoulder.

"Is there anything I can do to repay you for your generosity?" I asked.

"Yes," the shopkeeper said. "Avoid the same fate as my grandfather. You are young. Too young to risk your lives. Be careful and pay attention to the warnings. I will pray that my grandfather will watch over you."

"Thank you," Wyatt said. "You've been very kind, but we really must be going. Our expedition starts tomorrow."

"Travel safe," the shopkeeper said, raising his hand to us as we made our way back out the window.

"Thanks again," I said. "Your grandfather's piece is in good hands. I promise."

The shopkeeper nodded.

"See, Wyatt," I said as we climbed back onto the rusty balcony. "I told you that guy wasn't going to rip me off!"

Through the window, I could hear the shopkeeper laugh.

WYATT

FEBRUARY 24, 9:28 AM
CAIRO, EGYPT
17° CELSIUS, 63° FAHRENHEIT

This morning, I saw the Great Pyramids for the first time. There's almost no way to describe the feeling you get when you first take in a sight so amazing, but I'll try.

Waking again to the day's early morning call to prayer, I stepped onto the balcony. The sky was still dark. A handful of headlights zipped along the streets below, but for the most part the city was quiet.

Taking a deep breath, I rested my elbows on the railing and looked over the rooftops towards the desert. As the sun began to light the sky, a few shapes appeared just outside the city. Faint at first, then becoming more distinct, were three triangles. Two of them looked to be about the same size, with one much smaller triangle to the left. Almost hard to believe, but there before me was one of the seven ancient wonders of the world. The Great Pyramids of Giza!

The largest of the three, the Great Pyramid, was built by the Pharaoh Khufu around 2550 B.C. Originally 481 feet high, the Great Pyramid currently stands at 455 feet, thanks to years of erosion. It consists of 2.5 million limestone blocks weighing between 2.5 and 15 tons each, and covers over 13 acres of land. Archeologists believe that it took 23 years to build, which seems like a long time, but a simple calculation shows that the workers would have had to put one of these massive stones in place every few minutes, round the clock, to get it done in that amount of time. And that's just hard to comprehend.

The pyramid of Khafre, Khufu's son, was built to be slightly shorter than his father's, originally standing at 471 feet. Khafre also led the construction of the Great Sphinx of Giza. With the body of a lion and the head of a king, the Sphinx sits like a guardian at the base of Khafre's pyramid.

The pyramid of Menkaure is the smallest of the three, originally built to a height of 218 feet. To give some perspective, it's about one-tenth the total size of the Great Pyramid.

Even though we're not exactly sure how they were built, we do know why they were built, as burial chambers for the Pharaohs. In a way, they're kind of like the world's biggest tombstones.

"Gannon!" I said. "Get up! You have to see this!"

From somewhere under his covers, Gannon responded without flinching.

"I'm sleeping," he said.

"But the Great Pyramids are right outside our window!"

Again, Gannon didn't budge.

"I doubt they're going anywhere, Wyatt," he said. "I'll see them when I get up."

I shook my head.

"I have no clue how you won this fellowship."

"Skill, intelligence, and a long list of accolades," he said from under his covers. "That's how. Now let me get some more sleep!"

The Great Pyramids seen from Cairo

After a breakfast of eggs, potatoes, toast, and fresh-squeezed orange juice with our parents, the van arrived to take us to the marina on the Nile River where we'll board a boat to Luxor. In Luxor, we'll get first-hand experience exploring a tomb Dr. Aziz recently discovered. Dr. Aziz wants us to have a solid understanding of proper excavation techniques, and not learn the process at the expense of Cleopatra, which makes good sense. This tomb near the Valley of the Kings is his 99th discovery! What's inside, not even Dr. Aziz knows. Hopefully, we'll be the first to find out.

"You boys be safe," my mom said. "And make sure to keep an eye out for each other."

"We've got each other's backs," Gannon said, and smacked me hard on the shoulder. "Isn't that right, Wyatt?"

I glared at him without saying a word.

"I'll take that as a *yes*."

"Listen to me for a second," my mom said. "I can't emphasize this enough. I don't want you boys taking any unnecessary risks. You got it?"

"Come on, mom," Gannon said. "We're as cautious as a couple of mice at a cat farm."

Where Gannon comes up with these things, I have no idea.

"Good luck out there, boys," my dad said. "Whether you find anything or not, just have fun."

"That won't be a problem," I said.

"And try not to get yourself cursed," he added with a smirk.

"Don't even start, Dad," Gannon said.

"You better get going," my mom said. "You don't want to miss your boat."

"Ma'a Salama," Gannon said.

"Ma'a Salama," my mom replied.

"That means goodbye, Wyatt," Gannon said.

I rolled my eyes at him.

"You know, Arabic isn't as hard to learn as they say," Gannon said, sweeping his fingers across his shoulder. "A few more months here and I'd be fluent."

"How do you say 'that's a bunch of baloney' in Arabic?" I asked.

We all gave each other hugs, Gannon and I climbed into the van and the driver forced his way into traffic. We've been inching along for almost an hour now and cars are still backed up as far as we can see. Gannon's turning green from all the exhaust and keeps asking how much longer. Funny thing is, the driver always has the same answer: "Five more minutes!"

A Cairo mosque

GANNON

Sometime mid-morning we arrived at a downtown marina lined with rowboats and speedboats and lots of these traditional Nile sailboats called fellucas. Down at the end of the dock we found Dr. Aziz, James, and Serene and climbed aboard the river cruiser that's taking us to Luxor. It's an old wooden ship called the "River Queen." According to a man working on the boat, it has about a dozen cabins and holds around forty people total. He also told me the distance from Cairo to Luxor is "very far" and since this boat tops out at the speed of a canoe, we aren't going to get there until tomorrow afternoon.

Wyatt and I are sharing a cabin that's hardly bigger than a closet with a bunk bed crammed inside and no windows and nowhere to sit, so I've settled on the sundeck up top, which is wide open and without question the best place to take in the scenery along the Nile.

We're on our way and the sky is about as blue as it gets and the air on the river is definitely cooler than it is over land. As we cruised under a bridge just now, three Egyptian children leaned over the railing and waved to me from above. We've passed several larger riverboats docked along the banks and the famous Cairo Tower just went by on my left. All through the city, high-rise buildings crowd both shores. Most of them are gray and dust-covered and have billboard-sized neon signs on the roofs. Occasionally, I'll catch sight of a mosque, their big domes and minarets standing out from the rest of the concrete clutter.

Running along the western side of the river is a busy street all crammed with people walking every which way and backed up with traffic. Horns blast from everywhere, but they're far enough away that they don't really bother me. Looking around at the gridlock and chaos of the city only makes me more aware of how nice it is to be on a boat, cruising down this wide and peaceful river.

We're now moving beyond the city. The skyscrapers are fading into the haze behind us. Here, palm trees and farmland dominate the landscape instead of buildings and roads and cars. South of the city, most of the land is divided up into small, fenced-off plots where people farm. There are cows in some places, mostly thin with bones showing through their skin. There are men working these small plots of land, taking care of their crops, some with water buffalos pulling plows. There are also women in burkas and little kids helping in the fields. Other children are playing along the shore, some with dogs that are skinny like the cows.

Our boat is ignored by most adults, but the children always show interest. Whenever I wave they always wave back and shout and jump around with big smiles on their faces.

This is all so great out here on the river and I feel good and mostly relaxed, but I know the toughest part is ahead of us and I have to admit, nerves are starting to bubble up in my stomach again. My fear, I guess, is the unknown. Exploring unexplored tombs and all the dangers that go along with that kind of thing—the narrow tunnels and the dark chambers and the bats and rats, the snakes and booby traps, the curses and mummies . . . Jeez, I'm totally ruining this cruise by worrying about things that I might not even have to deal with.

I think it's time to put away the journal and enjoy the scenery. I mean, how many times in my life will I be aboard a boat cruising down the Nile River? I'm guessing, not many. If I can just ignore all these troubling thoughts, just put them out of my head completely, this cruise will be one of the memories of Egypt I'll cherish most.

Sunset over the Nile River

PART II

AN ANCIENT SECRET

WYATT

FEBRUARY 24, 10:56 PM
NORTH OF AL MINYA, EGYPT
24° CELSIUS, 75° FAHRENHEIT
SKIES CLEAR, WIND 5-10 MPH

Earlier tonight we learned of *Cleopatra's Secret.*

James, Serene, and I sat in the boat's dining area, playing cards as we moved south along the Nile. It was getting dark, as Gannon came down the steps from the boat's deck and joined us at the table.

"Be honest, mate," James said to me. "Do you really think we'll find Cleopatra?"

"Hard to say," I replied. "But I'm optimistic."

"But this is Dr. Aziz's sixth season excavating the site and he hasn't found anything that proves without a doubt that it's Cleopatra's burial place. What if he's made a mistake? Some archeologists believe he's digging in the wrong place. They say Cleopatra's tomb isn't anywhere near Alexandria."

"Don't you worry," Gannon said, "he's digging in the right place."

"How do you know?" James replied with sarcasm in his voice. "Did the Sun God, Ra, come down from the sky and give you this information?"

"Very funny," Gannon said. "Actually, Wyatt and I met a man whose grandfather was close to finding Cleopatra and he was digging in the northern deserts just outside Alexandria."

"So he said," I added, as a disclaimer. "We have no proof that what he told us is true."

"You'll believe just about anything won't you, mate?" James said to Gannon.

"I know it's true," Gannon said. "Check it out. He gave me this."

Gannon reached into his satchel and removed the relic the man had given him.

"See the profile," he said. "That's Cleopatra. The shop-keeper's grandfather found it near her tomb."

"Oh, he was a shopkeeper," James said. "That explains it. They'll tell you anything to sell their junk."

"It's not junk. Besides, he gave it to me. For free. Thought it might help us in our search."

"Can I see it?" Serene asked.

"Sure," Gannon said and handed her the relic.

Serene examined the piece. Running her thumb along the broken edge, she studied the profile.

"This is from the Ptolemaic period," she said, "which was the time of Cleopatra's reign."

"Oh, come on," James said. "Really?"

"Yes," she said with confidence. "I'm sure. We have a collection of relics from this period at the Egyptian Museum where I am interning. And this profile is very similar to other carvings of the Queen."

"Told you it was real," Gannon said with a smirk.

Serene leaned over the table, looking us each in the eyes.

"This is probably a good time to tell you," she said quietly. "There are a couple scholars who believe that Cleopatra went to her tomb with a powerful secret."

We all leaned in closer, gripped with curiosity.

"Not many people know this. It's kept top secret. I only know by accident. I was waiting outside Dr. Aziz's office one morning when he happened to be discussing it on the phone. He didn't know I was outside his door, and I don't want him to know. If this information got out, every archeologist in the world, not to mention every tomb robber, would soon be in Egypt digging up the desert. That's why you have to promise that you won't tell anyone."

"I promise," I said.

"I won't tell a soul," James said. "Cross my heart and hope to die."

"I won't either," Gannon said. "Your secret is safe with me."

"Do you know the story of the famous Library of Alexandria?" Serene asked.

"Yes," I said. "It was the greatest library in the ancient world. When Julius Caesar invaded Alexandria, he accidently set it on fire and destroyed all the material in the library."

"Not all," Serene said. "When Cleopatra learned the library was on fire, she sent several men from her army to save the most sacred texts. Luckily, they were successful. They brought these scrolls back to Cleopatra and she hid them from the Romans."

"What was in them?" James asked.

"Information that had been passed down among Egypt's Royal Historians for thousands of years. It's believed they explain some of ancient Egypt's greatest mysteries."

"Like what?" I asked.

"Like how the pyramids were actually built, the meaning behind their geometric dimensions, the significance of the Great Sphinx, and information on ancient curses, among other things."

"You're kidding?" James said.

"I'm just telling you what I heard," Serene said.

"Do the scrolls say anything about aliens?" Gannon asked.

I've come to expect off-the-wall comments from Gannon, but occasionally they are so far-fetched, even I'm taken by surprise.

"Aliens?" I said. "Really, Gannon?"

"I'm just asking. Some people believe extra-terrestrials played a part in building the pyramids. I'm not saying it's true, but you never know. The scrolls might say something about it."

"You sure do keep an open mind, don't you?" James said.

"Too open," I said.

"I don't know the exact contents of the scrolls," Serene said. "Just what I heard from Dr. Aziz, which is all speculation, really. Only Cleopatra knew. It was said that secrets contained in the scrolls were so powerful that Cleopatra ordered men loyal to her to bury them in her tomb at the time of her death and never tell anyone of their location. She was afraid that if the Romans took possession of the scrolls, they would be able to use the knowledge to expand their power and become an unbeatable force."

"This is incredible," I said.

"If it's true," James added.

"Just imagine," I continued. "Dr. Aziz said uncovering Cleopatra's tomb would be one of the greatest finds of the century. But to discover Cleopatra and the secret scrolls . . . that would be one of the greatest discoveries of all time!"

"Without question," Serene agreed.

I doubt I'll sleep much tonight. My mind is racing with thoughts of being part of the team that makes this discovery. I don't want to get ahead of myself, but I'm already picturing us on a world-wide museum tour. I can see it now. Stops in Tokyo and Los Angeles and Paris. Speaking in front of huge crowds. Cleopatra's treasures displayed all around us, as we provide answers to mysteries that have remained unsolved for thousands of years!

All right, calm down. One step at a time. Have to stay focused on the task at hand. First, Luxor and Valley of the Kings. Then Cleopatra. There's still lots of work to be done.

GANNON
FEBRUARY 25

The entrance to the tomb

We've gathered around the entrance of the tomb, which is just outside the city of Luxor, not far from the Valley of the Kings where the tomb of King Tut can be found, along with lots of other pharaohs. Luxor itself sits along the banks of the Nile. It's lush and green with flowers and ancient ruins everywhere you turn and there's no air pollution like in Cairo. Just outside the city is more desert with sharp, rugged mountains and canyons rising up in the distance. It's about as bright as the surface of the sun here and my eyes are squinted to tiny little slits and watering like a broken faucet. I have no clue how the ancient Egyptians worked in this valley without sunglasses.

"Welcome to A1," Dr. Aziz said, standing on the steps that lead into the tomb. "This is the 99th tomb I have discovered in Egypt, and the first in Luxor. We have been excavating this area for nearly four years. It wasn't until this last season that we discovered A1, which shows you the value of being persistent!"

Dr. Aziz went on to tell us that the "A" is short for Aziz, since it is Dr. Aziz who discovered the tomb, and that the "1" part came from the fact that it's the first tomb he has discovered in this area.

After Dr. Aziz's introduction, we got a lesson in excavation and learned some interesting archeological history. Here's something we learned that just seems idiotic to me. Back in the day, archeologists like Giovanni Belzoni used dynamite to blast their way into the chambers. I mean, really? Dynamite? Now, I'm no expert, but that's about as smart as burning down a forest to find an ivory-billed woodpecker. Goes without saying, but all that dynamiting destroyed some priceless ancient artifacts over the years.

Of course, the process has totally changed since then. Today archeologists go out of their way to prevent damage to the tombs. Dr. Aziz's men showed us a few modern excavation techniques using various tools and equipment and taught us how to tread lightly when on a dig. They also told us that we have to leave our cameras behind because the interior is so fragile that even something as harmless as a camera flash can cause damage.

Taking photos is not permitted in most tombs

Just as the lesson ended, two men came out of the tunnel and pulled Dr. Aziz aside. When he turned to us, he had a huge smile on his face.

"We happen to be here on a very special day," Dr. Aziz said. "My staff has just discovered a new passageway behind a large boulder. They are in the process of removing the boulder now and when they do, you will all have the privilege of being the first to explore the chamber."

Suddenly, this crazy fear rose up and gripped me tightly around the chest.

"I have a question," I said.

"Yes, Gannon?" Dr. Aziz answered.

"What's it like in there?"

"I cannot say for sure, but given my previous experiences, I'd say it's hot, dark, and narrow."

"That's what I was afraid of."

"What's the problem?" he asked.

"It's just that I tend to get claustrophobic in tight places."

"If you want to study archeology, you're going to find yourself in many tight places. That's part of the job. Did you not consider this when you applied for the fellowship?"

"You know, I didn't really think about it."

Wyatt rolled his eyes.

"Since when have you had a fear of small spaces?" he asked quietly.

"Since a few minutes ago."

"Toughen up, mate," James said. "This is just the kind of experience we all came here for."

"You'll be fine," Serene said. "Just stay calm."

Four men emerged from the tomb, all wearing surgical masks over their faces. One of the men removed his mask and spoke to Dr. Aziz in Arabic. When they were done talking, Dr. Aziz translated to us.

"The boulder has been withdrawn just enough for us to enter," he said. "But before we do, we will allow the chamber to breathe for a while. That will let the bad air out and the good air in. Then it will be safe."

"Seriously, Wyatt," I whispered. "I don't know about this."

"Look," Wyatt said, "Just think of it as a big hole in the ground. All we're going to do is walk inside and take a look around."

"But, no one has ever been inside this hole, which means no one knows what's down there. For all we know there could be booby traps. Jeez, I can see the headline now: Young Explorers Die After Being Hit by Poisonous Darts."

"You watch too many movies," Wyatt said. "Besides, we're with Dr. Aziz. What could go wrong?"

Famous last words, right?

Anyway, looks like I'm going in. Not that I really have a choice. Well, technically I do, but I can't exactly bail on our first archeological exploration just because I'm a little nervous. Dr. Aziz would scratch his head and wonder why the heck I even applied and he'd definitely be upset that I'd been picked when there were so many other qualified kids that deserve to be here.

Right now we're all just sitting around quietly in this blinding afternoon sun, waiting for all the toxic air to clear the tomb so we can poke around inside and get ourselves cursed . . . or worse!

WYATT

FEBRUARY 25, 3:56 PM
LUXOR, EGYPT, 25° 43′ N 32° 36′ E
25° CELSIUS, 77° FAHRENHEIT

Once the air cleared, we followed Dr. Aziz down a steep and narrow passage into the tomb, each of us holding a flashlight. Dust swirled in the beams as we moved deeper into the earth.

Dr. Aziz was like a little kid on his birthday.

"This is what makes my job so exciting," he said, hardly able to contain himself. "Remember, move slowly. You never know what we're going to run into down here."

"Um, what exactly *might* we run into?" Gannon asked.

"Follow me and we'll see."

Moving down the steps, I heard a strange sound. It almost sounded like a "hiss." Was my mind playing tricks on me? Was it just the sound of a boot sliding over the steps, or was it what I thought it was—a snake?

It was so dark I was having a hard time seeing anything clearly, even with the flashlight. I was disoriented. I couldn't keep my balance.

Then, I heard that sound again. It was a hiss. This time I was sure of it. From the corner of my eye, I caught sight of something moving within the stones. I stepped back slowly, careful not to make any quick movements. When I turned the flashlight on the wall, I saw the flutter of a narrow tongue as it lashed out. It was a snake, all right. Its beady eyes were staring right at me!

"Uh, there's a snake down here," I said, nervously pointing at the reptile. "It's coiled up right here in the stones."

"Just keep moving," Dr. Aziz said. "If you don't bother the snake, it probably won't bother you."

Honestly, his words weren't very reassuring. But, I did as he said and continued quickly down the steps, further underground.

We finally came to a narrow doorway that was partially closed off by a collapsed slab of stone. There was a small, square-shaped opening in the bottom. Dr. Aziz knelt down and shined his flashlight inside.

"Remarkable!" he said with so much enthusiasm you'd have thought he just found the Ark of the Covenant. "What a treat I have for you young fellows! Follow me!"

At that, Dr. Aziz crawled through the opening and disappeared. Gannon shined his flashlight on me.

"Is he serious?" he whispered.

"Of course he's serious."

"To be honest, I'd rather stay right here. I'm sorry, I've

tried to keep my mouth shut, but I'm feeling more than just a little claustrophobic."

"Dr. Aziz said he's got a real treat for us," James said. "Don't you want to see what's inside?"

Gannon thought for a moment.

"Fine," he said. "After you?"

"No, I insist," James replied. "You first."

"Suck it up," I said to Gannon.

"Yeah, mate," James added. "Dr. Aziz is waiting for us. Get in there."

Gannon shot us both an angry look, dropped to the ground and crawled into the opening. I know he wasn't happy, but there was no way I was going to let him turn back.

I followed close behind.

Through the collapsed doorway, the chamber opened up into a square room, probably fifteen feet at each side, with a ceiling just high enough for us to stand upright. I shined my flashlight along the ground in front of me, checking each step before I took it. Dr. Aziz was somewhere in the darkness. Then, suddenly, there was a click and a bright beam of light shot across the tomb.

"Behold!" he thundered. "Mummies!"

"Ooof!" James belted, and fell back into the wall as if he'd just been punched in the gut.

I was pretty startled myself. It's just not something you see every day.

"Amazing," Serene said.

"Judging by the tomb and the type of burial, this is probably a nobleman and his family," Dr. Aziz explained. "A mother, father, and the three mummies on the right are most likely their children. This is a brand new discovery and you are part of it!"

These mummies were wrapped in linen from head to toe, just like mummies I grew up seeing in cartoons. Because of these childhood memories, it wasn't hard for me to imagine them suddenly coming to life and attacking us.

What happened next was almost worse.

There was a low rumble and it seemed like the ground was giving way. The next thing I knew Gannon was falling, rock and dirt consuming him on all sides. When he came to a stop he was pinned, stuck in a narrow crack in the earth. One arm was wedged along his side. The other was raised over his head. He had fallen into a booby trap and couldn't move.

He fought, wiggled, thrashed, and screamed until his energy was all but drained. Dr. Aziz was yelling at him from above, but Gannon couldn't calm himself enough to hear what he was saying.

Finally, the words of Dr. Aziz registered.

"Stop moving or you'll be buried alive!" he screamed.

Gannon stopped.

Enough dirt had fallen into the shaft to bury him up to his chin. A small plume continued to slide into the shaft, slowly filling the hole. Gannon raised his chin, which gave him another inch between his mouth and the dirt. He whispered that his chest felt like it was being crushed and he was having trouble breathing.

Immediately, a rescue was underway. We only had minutes to save him. Dr. Aziz summoned the crew, who came running into the tomb with a cord of rope. The idea was to tie the rope under his arms and pull him from the hole. The problem was that his left arm was buried and there was no way to secure the rope around him. Instead the men used a small shovel and began carefully removing dirt from the hole.

"Gannon," I said calmly, "just try to relax."

"That's easy for you to say," he grunted. "You're not the one stuck in a booby trap."

The men were cautious in their movements, very aware that triggering a slide would bury Gannon completely. Little by little they cleared away enough dirt and debris to get the rope underneath his left arm. They then ran it around his back and under his right arm. The rope was secured with a double knot so that there was no chance of it coming undone once they started to pull him out.

The largest man in the crew took the rope in his hands and began to pull with everything he had, but Gannon didn't budge an inch. A second man helped. Still, he didn't move. So James, Serene, and I took the rope behind the men, as did Dr. Aziz. It felt like we were trying to pull Gannon from a pool of wet cement that had almost dried. He groaned in pain each time we pulled.

"Hang in there, Gannon," I said.

"I feel like I'm about to be torn in half," he said through clenched teeth.

"Try to wiggle yourself free as we pull," Dr. Aziz suggested.

We gave it one more heave and I felt Gannon being dislodged, freed of the dirt and pulled onto safe ground.

He was really shaken up. Sure, it was a pretty good scare, but I didn't think it would impact him as much as it has. When we got to camp, he took off on a walk and asked to be left alone. Serene just came into the tent and told me Gannon's considering leaving the fellowship. I'm hoping that's not true. I need to track him down and see what's going on.

GANNON

Okay, I'm sorry, but there's something about falling into a booby trap and almost being buried alive inside a tomb full of mummies that's a little hard to shake off. I honestly thought I'd be able to put it behind me when we got back to camp, but that just hasn't happened. I keep reliving that moment in my head. Even now, I can still feel the pressure of the earth closing in on me. I can still taste the dirt in my mouth.

I said it before and I'll say it again: I didn't consider just how dangerous this fellowship might be. And it sure as heck never dawned on me that my life would be at risk! Sure, I guess there's an element of danger in all travel, and definitely in all exploration, but if I had known just how hazardous this fellowship was going to be, I don't know if I would have applied in the first place. Here's the truth: After our experience at A1, I've had just about enough of archeology to last me a lifetime. And the problem is, we're just getting started.

When I told Wyatt I was leaving the fellowship and returning to Cairo, he tried to convince me to stay.

"You can't leave, Gannon," he said. "We're a team."

"Trust me, Wyatt, if there was any way for me to finish out this fellowship, I would. But you saw what happened to me in that tomb. Fear got the best of me and I totally froze up."

Wyatt took off his hat and wiped his forehead with his sleeve.

"Let's face it," I continued, "I'll be of no use on this expedition. I mean, despite what you think, I put a lot of work into my application and spent a lot of time studying, but I'm sure there are others who are more deserving. I probably shouldn't have won it in the first place. That's the part I feel most guilty about."

"You earned this fellowship. Give it some more time. In the end, you'll be happy you did."

I looked away, unable to face my brother.

"I have to get going," I said, and walked off to gather my things.

While I was packing my bags, Dr. Aziz entered the tent.

"May I have a word with you, Gannon?" he asked politely.

"Of course."

We each took a seat on a cot.

"I understand that this may be difficult for you," he said. "At your age, I would have been scared out of my mind at the thought of entering a tomb. And to find mummies inside, that probably would have sent me screaming for the exit."

"Really?" I said, surprised by this admission.

"I don't think I could have done it. It took me many years to get over my fears. Even today, I constantly have to remind myself why I am doing this."

"If you don't mind me asking," I said, "what is it that makes you so passionate about archeology?"

"It is my duty to uncover the mysteries of ancient Egypt," he said. "My duty to find these treasures and preserve them for future generations. This is Egypt's heritage. You must understand, there are thieves out there who will stop at nothing to find these artifacts before I do. These people care nothing of our history, our heritage. They have no desire to preserve these ancient wonders. They only care about money."

Dr. Aziz swept his arm over the desert.

"There are treasures hidden under these Egyptian sands worth a fortune. If the wrong people succeed in finding them before I do, it is likely that they will never be recovered, and thus, never truly understood. When we lose an ancient artifact, we lose a piece of our history . . . forever."

I felt ashamed that I had never taken the time to consider the real value of his work.

"The car is waiting to take you to the train station. If you wish to return to Cairo, I understand. Whether you stay or go, you must remember that you were given this prestigious fellowship for a reason."

"Wyatt said the same thing. But, I still can't help feeling like I've let everyone down."

"Few people your age have such an impressive resume. You don't acquire such a long list of achievements without possessing a great deal of inner strength. A person must be brave to do all that you have done. Do not forget that."

"Thank you, Dr. Aziz."

"No, thank you, Gannon."

Dr. Aziz stood up. He patted me on the shoulder and walked from the tent.

I sat on the edge of the cot for a long time, trying to decide what to do.

Stay or go?

The car was waiting.

I could hear the engine running.

I was driving myself crazy, sitting there thinking. I kept picturing myself in that booby trap, the dirt sliding in all around me. I couldn't take it anymore. To stay just seemed pointless. I needed to leave, slip out quietly, avoid goodbyes and all that. They'd be too difficult.

I grabbed my backpack and walked quickly to the car.

"We can go," I said to the driver, and climbed in the passenger seat.

As the driver pulled away from the site, I tried my best not to make eye contact with anyone in the camp. Still, I managed to catch sight of my brother out of the corner of my eye. He was standing there motionless, just watching us drive away, like he couldn't believe that I was actually leaving. As we came to the far end of the camp and turned onto the road, his head fell. To me, that said it all.

WYATT

FEBRUARY 26, 3:31 PM
32,471 FEET ABOVE THE DESERT
FLIGHT 523, EN ROUTE TO ALEXANDRIA

I wish I could say that Gannon returned last night. I wish I could write that he decided not to board the train to Cairo and instead took a car back to camp.

He didn't.

I've had a bad feeling in the pit of my stomach ever since he left. I like to think that I'm tough enough to handle any exploration on my own, but I've become used to my brother's company. We go everywhere together. Obviously, I've been taking him for granted.

"Gannon just isn't cut out for this kind of work," James said, after he left. "He's no explorer. Doesn't have the guts."

James had crossed the line, and I wasn't about to let him get away with it. I got right up in his face.

"You have no right to talk about my brother that way," I said. "You don't know anything about him."

"I know what I saw."

"He's twice the explorer you'll ever be!"

"Stop!" Serene shouted, stepping between us. "Both of you!"

I was furious, but stepped back to gather myself the best I could.

"We have a lot of work ahead of us," she continued, "and we'll have to function as a team if we hope to achieve our goals."

"Serene is right," I said. "And for that reason, I'm willing to put this behind us. But if I hear you say anything else about my brother, we're going to have a serious problem. You got that?"

James turned and walked away without answering, but I know he got the message.

"That kid can really boil my blood," I said, pacing the room.

"Forget about it, Wyatt," Serene said. "James sometimes speaks without thinking. You can't let it get to you."

"Easier said than done."

"I know it is. But we have to stay focused."

Since our experience in A1, tensions are high. It's safe to say that we're all really nervous about what we might encounter during our search for Cleopatra. Even Dr. Aziz has been on edge most of the day, which is understandable given all that's at stake. Basically, his reputation rests on the success of this mission.

Before we boarded the plane to Alexandria, I found Dr. Aziz seated in a far corner of the airport terminal, gazing out the window. There was an empty seat across from him.

"May I take this seat?" I asked.

"Please do."

I sat down and remained quiet, not wanting to disturb his thoughts. After some time, he spoke.

"Do you know that I have been excavating this site outside Alexandria for six seasons?"

"Yes, I was told."

"And that doesn't include the five years I spent building evidence that this was, in fact, the best place to search for Cleopatra's tomb. Eleven years, Wyatt. Eleven years of work focused primarily on this mission."

Dr. Aziz again turned his head to the window, as if questioning his long-term commitment. Then he leaned forward in his seat, resting his elbows on his knees.

"I have another question for you," he said. "A question that is very important for an aspiring scientist."

I leaned in, not wanting to miss a word.

"What do you think is the greatest challenge in the life of an archeologist?"

"That's hard to say."

He clinched his right fist.

"Overcoming doubt," he said with such conviction it was like he was trying to convince himself. "So much work and preparation go into choosing a location to excavate. Then you can spend years excavating. Of course, there are times when all of your work pays off and you make a wonderful discovery. Then there are times when you dig and dig and never find what you're looking for. This was the case in my search for the Pharaoh Nefertiti. We worked for years before realizing that there was nothing there. Only empty chambers. I must tell you, it is difficult to overcome such failings."

"But aren't you confident you're getting close to finding something at this site?" I asked.

"Finding something, yes. But therein lies the problem. What it is we'll find, no one knows."

"So you think Cleopatra might not be buried there?" I asked, regretting my question before I'd even finished asking it.

Dr. Aziz sat quietly for a moment. He turned his head and looked out the window.

"To give you an honest answer, Wyatt. I don't know. I just don't know."

GANNON
FEBRUARY 26
NIGHT

For me, Cairo has lost its magic. The frenzy, the chaos, and exotic charm of this ancient place, it's all been lost. But I know it's not Cairo. I mean, nothing has changed in the city. It's all me. I've changed.

My parents were waiting for me at the station when the train arrived.

"Hey, partner," my dad said. "Had a rough go of it, huh?"

"You could say that."

"Dr. Aziz called," my mom said. "He wanted to make sure you knew there was no shame in leaving the expedition. He said you are certainly not the first."

"Even Dr. Aziz has had panic attacks during his explorations," my dad said. "Just goes to show you, it happens to the best of them."

I know they meant well and all, but I was in no mood for a pep talk.

"Can you please take me back to the hotel?" I asked. "I'd like to be alone for a while."

"Sure," my mom said, and put her arm over my shoulder. "Let's go."

WYATT

FEBRUARY 26, 8:41 PM
TOMB COMPLEX OUTSIDE ALEXANDRIA, EGYPT
16° CELSIUS, 61° FAHRENHEIT
SKIES CLEAR, WIND CALM

We've settled into a camp made up of sixteen large tents. The camp sits high atop the desert dunes, approximately thirty miles southwest of Alexandria. James, Serene, and I are sharing a tent. It's very basic, with a cot and small desk for each of us, and there is a small bathroom attached. Dr. Aziz is outside inspecting the equipment with his assistant, Khalid, a 28-year old archeology student who is pursuing his doctorate. Our work begins tomorrow.

Camels carrying supplies through the desert

I can't stop thinking about the conversation I had with Dr. Aziz at the airport. Overcoming doubt. As he said, it's one of the greatest challenges an archeologist will face. Truth is, this applies to anyone who takes big risks. Being able to overcome doubt depends on a person's ability to stay the course when everyone else is ready to throw in the towel. But even strong willed people need "a little luck" every now and again. Reading the journals of some of the great archeologists, I've learned that they all struggled with doubt. Often-times, it was luck that pulled them through. Take Howard Carter, for example, who wrote the following in his book, *The Discovery of the Tomb of Tutankhamen.*

> "We had almost made up our minds that we were beaten, and were preparing to leave The Valley and try our luck elsewhere; and then— hardly had we set hoe to ground in our last despairing effort than we made a discovery that far exceeded our wildest dreams."

We could really use this kind of luck. We need to find something that will reassure Dr. Aziz that we are, in fact, digging in the right place. I'm optimistic, but this is all new to me. I haven't been digging here for six seasons like Dr. Aziz. It must be hard to remain positive year after year when you have almost nothing to show for your effort.

WYATT

FEBRUARY 26, 11:43 PM
TOMB COMPLEX, 30° 01' N   31° 13' E
14° CELSIUS, 57° FAHRENHEIT
SKIES CLEAR, WIND 5-10 MPH

By the light of a kerosene lantern, I've been reading all the material I could gather on the life of Cleopatra. I brought a book with me from home, and Khalid loaned me a binder of information to look over. If we're going to find the long lost Queen, I want to know everything I can about her.

Below is what I've learned so far:

Cleopatra was born around 69 B.C. She was of Macedonian descent and her name, in Greek, means "glory to her fatherland." She inherited the throne of Egypt at the age of eighteen and came to rule most of the eastern Mediterranean Coast. Cleopatra was educated in philosophy, politics, public speaking, and was fluent in nine languages.

Charismatic, cunning, and very intelligent, Cleopatra had a reputation as a formidable nemesis and ally. To say she was a strong woman is a huge understatement. She had relationships with two of the most powerful men in history—the Roman leader Julius Caesar, and the love of her life, the great General, Mark Antony. During the height of her reign, her wealth was unmatched in the world.

Throughout her life, Cleopatra had to fight for her power and many times she battled against her own family. Lying, cheating, banishment, assassination attempts, some successful, some not, Cleopatra definitely had a unique relationship with her relatives. Time and again, mothers fought wars against their sons, brothers against sisters, nephews against uncles.

Ultimately, Cleopatra was taken captive by her Roman rival, Octavian, and the end of her reign was all but guaranteed. Instead of letting her rival determine her fate, Cleopatra took her own life. Legend has it that she requested an asp be placed next to her in bed. She was soon bitten by the highly venomous snake and died not long after. Some believe she was buried with Mark Antony, who had died in her arms shortly before her own passing.

All right, it's getting late and we have some pretty tough days ahead. Time to extinguish the lantern and get some sleep.

GANNON

Last night was pretty much torture, thinking about the fellowship and all. Didn't sleep a whole lot. Tried, but couldn't. There were so many thoughts moving through my head that they got all backed up like the Cairo traffic.

Just after the sun was up, my mom walked into my room. Judging by the way she tilted her head and squinted her eyes, I must have looked like one of those mummies we found at A1.

"You feeling okay this morning?" she asked, concern in her voice.

"I've felt better," I said.

"I have an idea," she said. "I know you're interested in learning Arabic. I thought maybe you would enjoy helping me at the school today."

I sat up in bed and shrugged my shoulders. I mean, normally I would have been totally into something like that, but this morning I didn't feel like doing much of anything.

"Come on," she said. "It will be fun. The kids are great. You'll love spending time with them and they'll teach you some Arabic. What do you say?"

My dad had left for Giza before sunrise to work on his paintings, and it was obvious that sitting around the room wasn't going to do me a whole lot of good, so I agreed.

Downtown Cairo apartments

The cab dropped us off in front of a concrete building on a busy street a few blocks east of the Egyptian Museum. The building was dirty with pollution and in total disrepair. It had all kinds of Arabic signs hanging from it and there was this little tree standing in front of the building, just growing out of the sidewalk and covered in dust and looking all alone and sad in this congested, concrete jungle.

Inside the lobby, we made our way to the elevator.

"We're going to the fourth floor," my mom said.

I pressed the button and the doors opened. The elevator was the size of a tiny closet with a cracked mirror and a flickering bulb hanging from a wire in the center of the ceiling.

"Um, I think I'll take the stairs," I said.

"I'll join you."

Up the granite steps four stories was a yellow door.

"This is it," my mom said.

A wooden sign engraved in Arabic hung over the doorway. It looked like this:

مدرسه

"What does that say?" I asked my mom.

"School," my mom said.

"Can you spell it phonetically?"

"M-A-D-R-A-S-S-A-H."

When my mom walked in, the kids went wild, jumping up and down and clapping their hands and pulling on her dress. I wondered if teachers were always greeted like this, or maybe it was just that she was so different, tall and blonde and blue-eyed, a rare thing to see in the Arab world. Either way, I've never seen kids so excited to begin a day of school.

"Sabah el kheer," I said to the kids as they gathered around me. That means, "Good morning." I sat on the edge of the table and a boy climbed right up on my lap.

"Kaifa haloka?" I asked him. This translates to: "How are you?" when speaking to a male. When speaking to a female, it's "Kaifa haloki?"

Instead of answering, the kids would just smile and giggle and talk to one another, looking at me like I was the most curious thing they'd ever seen.

Their teacher was a young Egyptian woman who looked like she had just graduated from college. She came over and introduced herself.

"You must be Gannon," she said in perfect English. "I'm Mandisa Mahfouz."

"Pleasure to meet you," I said and we shook hands.

"Your mom has been a tremendous help. The kids are making great progress. As you can tell, they are thrilled to be learning how to read and write. Most of them will be the first in their family to do so."

The room was pretty simple with low ceilings and long cracks that ran all the way up the walls, most likely caused by the earthquakes that are common in Egypt. The windows along the far wall were open and you could hear the sound of the traffic below, only at a slightly lower volume because of the fourth-floor location.

None of these distractions mattered to the kids. They were there to learn. Ms. Mahfouz spoke to the class in Arabic and pointed to the blackboard where she had sketched the Arabic alphabet in bright white chalk. It looked like this:

ابجد هوز حطي كلمن

Abjad Hawaz Hotty Kalamon

The children read it aloud together as Ms. Mahfouz pointed to each letter. And just like that, the day was underway.

The literacy program was really something. I mean, not only were these children learning to read and write in Arabic, they were learning English as well, and the way they reacted to the lessons with such enthusiasm, well, it was just awesome.

I have to say, my time at the school was really fun, and under different circumstances I would have come back day after day to help, but something was eating away at me and when something is eating away at me so bad that I can't focus on anything else, there's only one thing to do, and that's to address the problem head on.

It was late afternoon and my mom and I were back on the sidewalk trying to hail a cab when I finally worked up the nerve to voice my feelings.

"I want to rejoin the fellowship," I said.

My mom looked at me and I could see what she was thinking. It was in her eyes. She was thinking that I was crazy. She was thinking that I'd probably just end up dropping out again when things got tough. She was thinking that I was setting myself up for another failure.

"Are you sure?" she asked. "Dr. Aziz said it's only going to get more difficult for the fellows. The complex outside

Alexandria is much more elaborate and built much deeper into the earth."

"I know, Mom. I'm not saying it's going to be easy, but I have no choice. I haven't stopped thinking about this since I left Luxor. I let Wyatt down. I let Dr. Aziz and the other fellows down. I can't live with that. I have to overcome my fears. I know I can do it. I've done it before."

"Well, Gannon, this is your call. You know your dad and I will support whatever decision you make."

"I've already made it, mom."

Tomorrow, I'm taking the first train to Alexandria and rejoining the expedition.

WYATT

FEBRUARY 28, 4:49 PM
TOMB COMPLEX
22° CELSIUS, 72° FAHRENHEIT
SKIES CLEAR, WIND CALM

At first, I thought I was seeing some kind of mirage. An optical illusion among the waves of heat. But, it wasn't a mirage. It was Gannon!

In typical grand fashion, he came riding up on the back of a camel, his desert scarf trailing off in the wind. The camel topped the dune and lumbered into camp. The man captaining the camel was wrapped in a long white robe and a kaffiyeh, a swath of material worn over the head. This man, I assumed, was a Bedouin, one of the nomadic tribesmen of the desert. He barked some orders and the camel knelt down, first on its front knees, then back, before coming to rest on its belly. Gannon slid off and paid the man his fare.

"Shokran, Abdulla," Gannon said, bowing his head.

Abdulla bowed in return.

"Well, look what the camel dragged in," I said.

Gannon turned to me and opened his arms to the desert.

"Call me, Gannon of Arabia!" he said, and flipped his scarf back around his neck.

I laughed.

"You have something against taxis?" I asked.

"Why take a taxi when you can take a camel?"

"You sure know how to make an entrance. I'll give you that."

"So, bring me up to speed. What's going on with the dig? Things look promising?"

"When Dr. Aziz arrived the excavation kicked into high gear. We've already managed to clear away lots of sand in the two areas where he thinks there might be a chamber. We haven't found anything yet, but he's pretty sure we will. It's just a matter of time."

"So," Gannon said, "this is really happening, isn't it?"

"It is. And here's the best part. Not only are we part of the dig, we're on the front lines. If there's a find, we're going to be right there. You made a great choice coming back. This fellowship is incredible!"

I held a pickaxe in my hand.

"Dr. Aziz lets you walk around with that thing?" Gannon asked, pointing.

"I told you. We're on the front lines."

"I might have to question Dr. Aziz's judgment on that one."

Gannon hopped up on a flat stone and surveyed the complex. The uniformed men caught his attention.

"Who are all the guys with guns?" Gannon asked.

"The Egyptian military police. They're here to protect the site."

Gannon stared at the policeman nearest us. Like all the other military police, he wore a black suit, black boots with white gaiters and a red beret. Each member of the police squad carried an AK-47 submachine gun and had a pistol on their hip.

"That's some serious protection," Gannon said. "You think it's totally necessary?"

"I guess so. Who knows what kind of treasure might be buried at this site? I'm sure there are tomb robbers out there who would love to get their hands on it."

Gannon didn't say anything for a minute. He just looked around the site, adjusted his scarf.

"Gannon!" came a booming voice. "I had a feeling you wouldn't be able to stay away!"

Dr. Aziz jogged to my brother and gave him a hug.

"I'm here for good this time," Gannon said. "That, I promise."

"Very happy to hear it."

"So put me to work. If memory serves, we're searching for a Queen. Is that right?"

Dr. Aziz laughed and the two of them walked off toward the excavation site.

Sure, Gannon can drive me nuts sometimes, and I'm already anticipating more drama now that he's rejoined the fellowship, but all that said, I couldn't be happier to have my brother back. An adventure like this wouldn't be the same without him.

Desert transportation

GANNON
LATE NIGHT

By way of train, foot, and camel, I arrived at the excavation site and found the place bustling with activity. From the hilltop it looked almost like a colony of ants, just with men instead of ants, all carrying shovels and pickaxes and carting away piles of rock and debris. I broke a sweat just watching them.

Well, with all this going on, Dr. Aziz wasted no time putting me to work. This afternoon I probably shoveled enough sand to build my own pyramid. My back aches. I can hardly lift my arms. My hand shakes as I write. But I'm not complaining. At least, not out loud. I'm here to redeem myself and will do whatever's asked of me with a huge smile on my face!

WYATT
MARCH 1, 11:28 AM
TOMB COMPLEX
21° CELSIUS, 70° FAHRENHEIT
SKIES CLEAR, WIND 5-15 MPH

We've just made an amazing discovery! Three steps buried in the sand! And more below it, I'm sure. A workman on break found the steps when he tossed his shovel aside and heard it hit something hard. Now, that's luck, pure and simple. But, hey, like I said, we'll take it.

Right now the men are clearing away the rubble. The

plan is simple. Follow the steps and see where they lead. Dr. Aziz has also ordered radar scans of the area to see if there might be a tunnel or chamber underground.

The military police have taken a serious interest in our work. Several of them are huddled around the steps, closely monitoring our progress. Earlier, Dr. Aziz had an argument with the police commander. I wasn't sure what they were shouting about, since they were only speaking in Arabic, but it was pretty heated. When I asked Dr. Aziz if everything was all right, he acted as if there was nothing to worry about, but it's obvious there's some tension between them.

GANNON
MARCH 2

We reached the fifteenth step and have started to clear the area around the walls that run down either side of the staircase, which are carved up with all these cool hieroglyphics. At first Dr. Aziz got really excited about the carvings, thinking that maybe they'd tell us something about Cleopatra, so he went right to work copying down and translating everything. Of course, I convinced myself the hieroglyphics were some kind of curse, the kind that says, "A swift death will come to all who enter this tomb," or some horrible thing like that.

Turns out it was a message to Osiris, the ruler of the

afterlife. Dr. Aziz was a little upset it wasn't something more specific. He's anxious to find some kind of proof that this is really Cleopatra's tomb.

Okay, that's all for now. I need to grab a quick snack, chug some serious water, and get back to the dig.

Egyptian carvings

WYATT

MARCH 3, 7:57 PM
TOMB COMPLEX
32° CELSIUS, 90° FAHRENHEIT
WIND 70 MPH, GUSTS TO 90 MPH

This morning, the sky turned blood red on the horizon.

Dr. Aziz ran from his tent with Khalid and they climbed to the top of a dune to assess the approaching storm.

"I'm afraid this may be worse than the meteorologists predicted," he said. Then he turned to the crew and shouted orders. "We must make sure the camp is secure enough to hold when the winds arrive! Everyone hurry! The storm will be here soon!"

We all went to work, checking the ropes and stakes that held our tent camp to the desert floor. Most of the support ropes were grounded by large rocks, some weighing as much as fifty pounds.

Soon, a purple and red haze reached from one end of the horizon to the other, like a wall of sand slowly consuming the earth. Storms like this are not uncommon in these parts. They come off the Mediterranean Sea, picking up desert sand and dust as they roar eastward. I had read that these storms are sometimes bad enough to bring all outdoor activity to a halt, forcing people to take shelter until they pass. But even reading of such accounts, I wasn't at all prepared.

"Everyone to your tents!" Dr. Aziz shouted. "The storm is nearly upon us!"

I was putting one last rock over a stake supporting the kitchen tent, when a strong wind charged up the hill from the west. The wind was hot, like a wind coming off a distant forest fire, and carried with it a thick plume of sand. I lifted my scarf over my mouth and turned my back to the wind. The sand hit the exposed skin on my forearms like tiny needles. At first I thought the initial gust would ease enough for me to gather my things and run inside the tent. But the wind didn't let up. Actually, it increased, blowing harder and moving up the dune with such force that it pushed me back a few steps. I had to squat down to keep from being blown over.

Visibility was no more than a few feet. Through the thundering wind, I could hear shouts of men and see the occasional worker making a break for his tent. The wind continued, refusing to let up, even for a second. I needed to get to shelter.

Staggering, half-blind, my arm bent around my eyes to shield them from the driving sand, I found our tent and quickly made my way inside. Gannon, Serene and James were seated on the floor in the center of the tent.

"Sorry, I didn't want to say it," Gannon shouted, "but I'm starting to think we're cursed!"

Serene remained silent.

"It's just a sandstorm!" I yelled.

"No, this is not *just* a sandstorm!" Gannon shouted back. "It's the mother of all sandstorms! Listen to that wind! The whole camp's going to blow away! We'll be buried alive! Just like the shopkeeper's grandfather!"

"The tent will hold!" I yelled, though I wasn't so sure.

The inside perimeter of the tent is lined with heavy rocks for added support. With all of that weight, it will take a tornado to blow our tent away, but the wind is pounding at the canvas walls with such force, I'm afraid it might rip apart at the seams.

"I never thought I'd say this," James said, "but I'm with Gannon! Maybe we got too close to the tomb and now we're cursed!"

Serene has not spoken, but there is fear in her eyes.

I'm not buying into the curse theory. Fact is, a desert storm is upon us and we're helpless to do anything, but wait it out.

GANNON
MARCH 5

For two days and two nights this storm has raged. I've never seen anything like it! By some miracle, the tent has managed to hold up somehow, but the constant battering has definitely taken its toll. Last night a rip appeared in one of the corner seams and started to grow with each rush of wind. We were scared that the tear might open more and if that happened the entire roof would be blown off, so we raced around looking for anything that could be used to patch it up. What we ended up doing was using a pocket knife to cut a slit into the canvas on either side of the tear, then we taped a couple pens and pencils together, pushed them through the slits, and twisted them around until the tear was tightly closed off.

So far, it has held.

The sound of the wind whipping against the tent has us all on the verge of a breakdown. I'm not joking, it's like a thousand drums pounding in our ears all at once . . . for days on end! And to make matters worse, we haven't slept now since before the storm hit. The air inside the tent is terrible and hot and swirling with dust, making it really hard to breathe. My outlook on this whole thing isn't good and I'm not the only one.

"I can't take it anymore!" James yelled, as he paced the inside of the tent.

"Stay calm, James!" Serene yelled. "There is nothing we can do!"

"All this noise! It's driving me crazy!"

I thought he'd totally lost it and was afraid he'd run out into the storm and never be seen again. But Serene came up with a great idea and grabbed two pillows from a cot and handed them to James.

"Lay down and put these over your ears!" she yelled.

James took the pillows and dove onto the cot and pressed them over his head.

That's when I heard someone pounding at the door.

"Open up!" a voice shouted from outside. "It's Dr. Aziz!"

I quickly undid the knot and opened the canvas flap. Sand started pouring in so fast I could hardly see. Dr. Aziz jumped through and we quickly closed the flap. He had a small plastic container with some food and a jug of water.

"Here's some food and water to get you through the night!" he shouted over the wind. "I just got a radio call! The storm should pass by morning!"

"I hope so!" I yelled. "We're going crazy in here!"

Dr. Aziz noticed James lying on the cot with pillows pressed over his head.

"Is James going to be okay?" he asked.

"He'll be fine!" Wyatt said. "How's the rest of the camp holding up?"

"A few tents have been destroyed! I'm not sure how much longer the other tents will last! I'll check in tomorrow morning! I have to get supplies to the other men!"

Dr. Aziz left and I think I'm going to join James and ride out the rest of this storm with pillows over my ears. This wind is driving me absolutely insane!

WYATT

I woke to an eerie silence. The wind had stopped. The dust had settled.

Serene, James and Gannon were all asleep, everyone with pillows over their heads. It felt like I was waking from a terrible dream. My head was throbbing, my ears ringing. My lungs burned with each breath. Our tent leaned awkwardly to one side. The support poles were twisted and bent. The roof had collapsed and was slumped in the center.

The air was cold. Colder than it has been any morning since we arrived. Stepping from the tent, I pulled my jacket closed, buttoned it up over my neck, and went walking around the site.

Outside, everything had changed. The camp was torn apart. Drifts of sand, some as high as twenty feet, stood where tents used to be.

The sun was just peeking over the eastern dunes as I walked in the direction of the steps. When I got to where I thought they had been, I looked around, but saw nothing. Everything we have worked so hard to uncover, the staircase and walls that might very well have led to Cleopatra's tomb, it's all been buried by the storm. Lost in the desert. Almost as if it never existed.

A camel after the storm

GANNON

After experiencing a storm like that, it's a miracle archeologists ever find anything in this desert. I mean, it consumed the excavation site whole, concealing everything under deep hills of sand.

Serene said we were lucky, that it could have been worse, which is really hard for me to believe, but apparently this storm was minor compared to the storm Egyptians fear most. It's called a "Khasmin" and it packs 100+ mile-per-hour winds and can last for 50 days! I can't even imagine.

The decision now is whether to continue the dig or abandon this place altogether. After this whole ordeal, I can't help but think that maybe there's a reason Cleopatra has never been found. Maybe she's not supposed to be found. Maybe her secrets are meant to remain just that—secrets, for eternity!

WYATT
11:27 AM

When we entered Dr. Aziz's tent this morning, we found him pacing.

"This isn't it," Dr. Aziz was saying to himself. "This isn't the place."

We all looked at each other, not sure how to react.

"All those years of work, and I've got it all wrong."

"How could you say that?" Serene asked.

"If we'd found any evidence this was the place, we would forge ahead," he said. "However, I'm afraid Cleopatra is not here."

"But all of your research led you to this location," I said. "And we've found the steps."

"We have no proof that there will be anything of significance down those steps. The chambers we've seen on the radar appear to be empty."

"But they may not be," I said.

"I'm telling you, we are in the wrong place. This is just like my experience in the Valley of the Kings when I was certain I had found the burial place of Nefertiti. Once again, I've made a terrible mistake. I must stop this excavation at once."

He then stormed across the tent and disappeared out the door. We just sat there, quietly looking at each other.

What happens now, I don't know, but I'm afraid the fellowship may be coming to an end.

WYATT

12:13 PM

Khalid just informed us that the military police are insisting the excavation continue, regardless of what Dr. Aziz says. Why they are being so adamant that we continue, I'm not sure; but it does make me question their motives. Dr. Aziz argues that he is in charge and the decision is not theirs to make. Outside, tensions are growing. People are arguing with one another and there's all sorts of shouting. I'm honestly worried things are going to spiral out of control.

The military police

GANNON

Lots of the workers were taking down tents and packing up tools and equipment, while the military police yelled and pointed guns at everyone, demanding they get back to work. To tell the truth, I don't trust these guys at all, but there was really nothing I could do so I just started jogging away, wanting to remove myself from the whole mess.

I climbed a far dune and walked down the back side until I couldn't see or hear the camp anymore and then continued into a small valley between the dunes and just sat there for a while, trying to clear my head.

Several dust clouds swirled in the wind, spinning across the desert floor like a crazy band of Tasmanian Devils. My shoes were filled with sand so I took them off and dumped it out and walked around barefoot for a while. The sand was new, almost cool, just put down by the storm and not yet baked by the sun.

Walking through this valley, looking up at the dunes on either side, I was caught by surprise when my foot struck a hard object. Wow, did it hurt and I hopped around on one leg a few times and finally fell back into the sand, thinking for sure that I'd cut it wide open. I brushed away the sand from my foot and breathed a huge sigh of relief at finding only a small scratch near the arch.

I was putting my boots back on when I noticed what I'd stepped on. The edge of a long, flat stone buried in the sand. I knelt down and carefully brushed off the sand, exposing a rectangular slab with etchings across it. Because of the storm I couldn't tell where anything had been and wondered if this stone was part of the same complex we'd been excavating or if it was some completely different section that Dr. Aziz didn't even know about.

I kept scooping sand away and suddenly it started to give and sink down beneath the stone, almost like sand falling through an hourglass. I scrambled backwards on my hands to keep from being sucked down with it and watched as more of the stone was revealed. When the sand finally stopped, one side of a large entryway stood before me with all kinds of elaborate carvings on it. I stood up to take it all in and that's when my eyes caught sight of something I could hardly believe.

On one side of this stone slab was a grouping of smaller tiles, each carved with the same design. After focusing on it for a moment, I could make out the carving. It was the profile of a human face. A woman's face!

A chill ran through my arm as I reached into my satchel to retrieve the piece from the shopkeeper. When I compared the two, looking at one and then the other and back again to make absolute sure my eyes weren't playing some kind of trick on me, I almost fell over.

I gathered my footing and ran back towards the camp as fast as I could.

"Stop!" I yelled. "Everyone stop packing up!"

The men's shouting quieted and everyone turned to see what I was yelling about. Khalid and Dr. Aziz came out of their tent.

"We can't leave," I said, trying to catch my breath. "We have to stay."

"I'm sorry," Dr. Aziz said, "I've given orders. We are to abandon the excavation at once."

"No," I said, trying my best to ignore the nerves that had my stomach doing flips. "We can't abandon the dig!"

"Unless you have good reason to do otherwise," Dr. Aziz said, "we're departing before nightfall."

"Listen to what the boy has to say!" the military police commander shouted, his arms resting on the barrel of his machine gun.

Everyone went dead silent. I swallowed my fear and spoke.

"We're in the right place," I said. "Cleopatra is here. I'm sure of it."

"How can you be certain?" Dr. Aziz asked.

"I'll show you. Come with me."

We all went up and over the dune and came down into the valley where the entryway stood.

"What is this?" Dr. Aziz said quietly to himself.

"Many years ago, there was a man who came close to finding Cleopatra's tomb," I said. "His name was Rifa'a Kamil."

Dr. Aziz returned his eyes to me.

"I know of this man, Kamil," Dr. Aziz said. "He was an archeologist."

"That's right."

"If I remember correctly, he went into the desert one season and was never found."

"Yes!" I said. "This very desert! We met his grandson in Cairo and when I told him that we were going in search of the Queen, he gave us a relic that had been given to him by his grandfather."

I held out the piece. Dr. Aziz took it in his hand and ran his thumb across the profile.

"Now look at the etchings on the entryway," I said. "See the center tile?"

Dr. Aziz moved closer and squinted his eyes. He did a double-, then a triple-take.

"Unbelievable," he said to himself. "Truly unbelievable."

A smile crept up one side of his face, as he continued to compare the etching on the piece with the one on the entryway. We all held our breath, waiting for him to speak. Finally, he looked up at everyone.

"Despite our recent progress," Dr. Aziz said, "I have been plagued by many doubts. Even finding the steps did not ease my uncertainty. I've found steps like this before that have led to nothing. Three others at this site alone. I was beginning to think that my time was up, that maybe I would never discover my 100th tomb."

Again, Dr. Aziz looked at the relic.

"Are you confident this man was truly the grandson of Rifa'a Kamil?" he asked.

"I am," I said.

Dr. Aziz clinched the relic in his hand and gazed up at the sky, like he was trying to communicate with the heavens or something. Then he looked out over the crew.

"My friends!" he shouted, "I believe we have been delayed long enough!"

"Does that mean we're continuing the excavation?" Serene asked.

"We have no choice," he said with a smile. "History depends on us."

WYATT

MARCH 7, 12:07 AM
TOMB COMPLEX
16° CELSIUS, 61° FAHRENHEIT
SKIES CLEAR, WIND 5-10 MPH

To find a piece that was so similar to the one the shopkeeper gave to Gannon, well, the odds are astronomical. It's just like that donkey whose foot fell through the hole at the Valley of the Golden Mummies, but this time, instead of a donkey it was Gannon, which, come to think of it, is pretty much the same thing.

I do have an issue with Gannon's theory that this relic is *proof* that Cleopatra is here. All it really proves is that this is the location where the shopkeeper's grandfather was digging for the Queen. But, there's no proof that the shopkeeper's grandfather was digging in the right place. He disappeared, so no one really knows.

As an aspiring scientist, I'm always looking for undeniable proof. Even though I don't agree with the decision-making process, which is basically "ignore all logic and go with your gut," I'm with Gannon and Dr. Aziz. It seems much of what an archeologist does is based on gut instinct. Besides, who am I to argue with a man who has discovered 99 tombs?

We've come this far. To give up now would be wrong.

The discovery of the entryway was not enough to convince everyone to stay. Because of the storm, some believe that a curse is upon us and that anyone who continues working is in danger. There was no changing their mind. In total, seventeen men left camp today. Before they did, they all apologized personally to Dr. Aziz.

This did not discourage him in the least. In fact, he respected their decision.

"These beliefs have been passed down for centuries and cannot be discounted," he said.

Since we now have a much smaller crew, Dr. Aziz ordered new radar scans taken of the tomb complex and for all of the hallways and chambers to be outlined in the sand with strings and flags.

Everyone who stayed was far too excited to just stand around. It was getting dark, so we brought in floodlights and took up shovels and started clearing more of the entryway. This went on well into the night, before Dr. Aziz ordered everyone to get some rest.

I'm seated at the desk inside the tent, writing by

candlelight. Everyone else is asleep. I should be sleeping, too. It will be light in a few hours and the next few days are sure to be long.

GANNON
MARCH 9
NIGHTTIME

There's been lots of good progress since the storm. We're now beyond the entryway and are carefully removing sand and rock using these smaller hand-shovels and brushes so that we don't damage any of the stonework.

I haven't been able to write a word in my journal for almost two days now. I mean, I've been so whipped I could hardly lift a spoon to my mouth or water to my lips, much less pick up a pen and scribble in my journal. My hands are raw and blistered and throbbing like they have their own heartbeat.

Our evenings go pretty much like this:

When we finish our work we head to the dining tent for rice and beans or falafels with flat bread and some hot tea. After eating, I don't even have the energy to wash up and usually just stumble into the tent and collapse onto my cot, still wet with sweat and covered in sand. I'm always sleeping like a mummy within seconds and that's a good thing because it doesn't give my brain much time to think about curses and all.

Okay, I'm falling asleep at the desk. Time to hit the cot and catch some Zs.

WYATT

9:32 PM

This afternoon we uncovered two intricately carved limestone pillars. The crew is very tired and we're working a little slower today. Personally, my shoulders and back are in serious pain.

It's been tough going, but no one wants to stop. I have volunteered, along with the other fellows and most of the crew, to work another two-hour shift ending at midnight. After some sleep, those of us who are able will wake, wash up, eat a quick breakfast and return to work. The first shift tomorrow begins at 5:00 AM.

Pillars at the tomb complex

GANNON

Okay, being cursed isn't my biggest fear anymore. I mean, I'm still worried about it, for sure, it's just not my biggest concern. What concerns me most are the military police.

With their dark uniforms and unfriendly faces and huge guns, they're totally intimidating, no way around it, and even though I've been skeptical about these guys from day one, up until now I haven't said much. But tonight after dinner, I had to go and open my big mouth.

"Excuse me," I said, catching the commander as he walked past. "I'm just curious. What exactly are the police doing here?"

He stopped dead in his tracks.

"I'm sorry, young man?" he said, locking his eyes on mine. "What did you say to me?"

I gulped, and asked again.

"I was just wondering why we need so much security?"

Questioning this man, I realized right away, was a huge mistake.

"We are working in the interest of the Egyptian people," he said. "We are here to protect the antiquities from tomb robbers. We are here to make certain that the country's heritage is preserved."

The volume of his voice increased with each sentence making it pretty clear that he wasn't too happy with me.

"And who are you to question my purpose?" he asked.

"I'm sorry," I said timidly. "I didn't mean it like that. It was just a simple question."

"You are a foreigner. I should be skeptical of you. What exactly is your purpose?"

I was nervous now and began to stammer.

"Oh, well, uh . . . I'm one of the winners of the Youth Exploration Society fellowship," I said. "I'm here with Dr. Aziz."

I'd hoped that dropping Dr. Aziz's name would make the commander cool off and leave me alone. It didn't.

"Fellowship or not," he said, "I see you as an intruder. There is a long history of foreigners raiding this country for its ancient riches. Why should you be any different?"

"No, I wouldn't, uh, I'd never . . ."

I was scared. Fumbling my words. I couldn't complete a sentence.

"Did you know that in ancient times tomb robbers faced *brutal* consequences if they were caught?" he asked.

I shook my head.

The man moved closer to me and lowered his voice.

"They were sacrificed in the same way an ox was sacrificed to the gods. Cut open and left to bleed. Then, their bodies were burned. This was the ultimate punishment. Having their bodies turned to ash. After death, they could not be reborn."

The commander put his hand on my shoulder and all the air went out of me. I literally couldn't breathe.

"If I were to catch a tomb robber today," he continued, "I would not go to the trouble the ancient authorities went to."

"No?"

"No," he said, shaking his head. "I would simply shoot them on the spot."

"I'm not here to rob the tombs," I said, my voice trembling. "I promise."

"So you say," he continued. "But I have no reason to trust you. In my eyes, you are guilty until proven innocent."

"I better go check in with Dr. Aziz," I said, searching for a way out.

"This conversation never happened," he said, sternly. "Do you understand?"

"Yes," I said, staring down at the sand.

"Look at me!" he shouted.

I raised my eyes to him. His stare was cold. His jaw rippling.

"I will be watching you," he said. "Do not make a mistake."

I nodded, but dared not move. He spit into the sand and finally dismissed me with a wave of his arm. At that, I took off running for my tent.

I am totally freaked out right now! I mean, I don't feel safe at all. Really, I don't even know what to do. I'm afraid if I mention this to anyone my life might be in danger. I don't even think I should say anything to Wyatt. It might put him at risk, too. Jeez, this is crazy! All I can really do is hope that Dr. Aziz becomes suspicious on his own, and sets things right with these guys.

WYATT

Exactly 22 feet into the entryway we've found carvings that suggest that this is, in fact, a royal burial chamber!

More ancient carvings

Just beyond these carvings is a massive stone slab that's preventing us from going any further into the tunnel. More debris is being removed so that a proper survey can be conducted. The engineers are meeting with Dr. Aziz and Khalid to decide the best way to move the stone without damaging the tomb.

Have to rest before work continues.

GANNON

Okay, I'm only writing now to distract my brain and keep it off the military police and the fear of being cursed and every other potential crazy thing that could go wrong.

So, here's the status of the dig:

When we were clearing all the sand and rock from around the giant stone that's blocking the hallway, a crack was found in one of the pillars. Dr. Aziz said it had probably been damaged by the earthquakes that have rocked this area over the centuries. The cracked pillars created this small triangle-shape opening in the upper right corner of the entryway, about twelve feet off the ground.

Wyatt climbed to the top of the scaffolding and measured the triangular crack. It's just large enough for one of us to squeeze through, but it's packed tightly with all kinds of rubble. A bunch of men are working to clear it out so we can take a look inside. Dr. Aziz asked that any hieroglyphics be copied down on a notepad and brought to him right away. He's now looking for a name or something carved into the stone that would tell us without a doubt the person or persons who were buried here. I'm pretty sure he still agrees with me that this is Cleopatra's tomb. I mean, he did resume the dig after we found the matching tile and all, but until he's got some kind of absolute proof, he's being real careful not to say anything.

Okay, break time's over.

Focus on the task, Gannon.

Don't let your brain wander.

Everything will be fine.

You can do this!

WYATT

2:14 PM

Beyond the opening in the stone it was dark. Khalid handed me a flashlight. I crawled further inside and turned it on.

"What do you see?" Khalid asked.

It looked like there was a shaft that opened up to my left, just behind the stone slab. That was the only open space. Other than the shaft, there was only rubble, piled from floor to ceiling.

"I can't see very much," I told him. "Just lots of rock and dirt."

I continued to scan the interior for clues. Barely visible above a pile of rocks, I saw a set of hieroglyphics inscribed on a slab.

"Hand me a pencil and notebook," I said to Khalid. "There's an inscription inside."

I made a sketch of the hieroglyphics and Gannon ran them to Dr. Aziz's tent for translation. Here is a copy:

Right now, I'm resting in the shade, waiting for the translation.

GANNON

Dr. Aziz stared at what Wyatt had drawn in his notebook for quite a while. He looked at me then back to the notebook without saying a thing. At first I thought it must not have been anything too important, when all of a sudden he leapt from his chair and went sprinting out of the tent, yelling like a madman. I tried to catch up. When he got to the entryway he stopped and bent over to catch his breath.

"Would anyone care to guess what this says?" he asked, still panting, as he held up the inscription of the hieroglyphics.

"If it's a curse," James said, "I'd rather not know."

"No, it does not say anything about a curse," Dr. Aziz said.

"What does it say then?" I asked.

"My friends, it says . . . Cleopatra! This is it! We've found the tomb of the Queen!"

Everyone at the camp went wild, cheering and jumping around and hugging each other. I came back to the tent to get my video camera. I mean, I knew this was it, totally, but now that it's officially-official, I'm totally freaking out!

Wow, so, I guess we'll be meeting the famed Pharaoh real soon. I should probably get back out there and document the occasion. I mean, this right here is history in the making!

PART III

THE SEARCH FOR EGYPT'S LAST PHARAOH

WYATT

What happened after Dr. Aziz confirmed that it was, in fact, the tomb of Cleopatra is as great a tale as Howard Carter's discovery of King Tut. However, our story has a very different outcome.

Let me explain . . .

Our celebration was cut short, interrupted by the explosive sound of gunfire, as the military police shot their rifles into the air. They then turned their guns on the crew. The commander climbed to the top of the scaffolding and spoke in Arabic. His voice was stern and authoritative. The workers quietly shared glances with one another.

After the commander finished, he spoke to us in English.

"For those of you that do not speak Arabic," the commander said, "I will give you the abbreviated version in English. From this point forward, you all will do as I say, no questions asked. You obey my orders, and I will allow you to live. If you try to escape or disrupt our operation in any way, you will be dealt with swiftly. We are not interested in preserving the integrity of this tomb. We are only interested in the treasure that is buried inside. And since time is of the essence, we are going to blow up this stone slab with dynamite."

He lowered his gun on me.

"First, we need the young fellows working with Dr. Aziz to crawl through this opening and tell us what they see inside. If the treasure is just behind this wall, we will have to use less dynamite so we do not destroy it. If it is deeper inside the tomb, we will blast the wall to pebbles."

"It's not safe to explore inside," I said, my voice shaky. "The structure is not secure. The whole thing could collapse while we're in there."

"That is not my problem," the commander said coldly. "But for your sake, we will hope that it holds."

Being forced through a tiny crack into a crumbling tomb at gunpoint was like a nightmare coming true. James buckled under the pressure. When he reached the top of the scaffolding, he started shaking and suddenly dropped to his knees.

"I can't do it," he said. "I can't go in there."

When the men tried to lift him, he fought like a man being sent to his death. Finally, the commander stepped in.

"Forget this one," he said. "Take him away. We will just send the other three."

James was forced from the scaffolding, tied up, and dragged, kicking and screaming, across the sand towards the camp. I was afraid we would never see him again.

"You others get inside!" the commander said. "I expect detailed notes of your findings. And you, with the camera," he said to Gannon. "Take video of what you find. I want the truth. Try to fool me, and I will line you up in front of a firing squad."

I went in first. My chest tightened as I squeezed through the crack, pulling myself forward on my stomach across the sandy stone. Once inside, I braced myself against the wall and dropped to the ground.

It was dark and dusty. I turned on the flashlight and set it atop a flat stone so I could help the others climb down. All three of us were now behind the stone slab that was put in place thousands of years ago to keep people out. Flashlights in hand, we moved over the rubble, further into the tomb. The hair on the back of my neck stood on end. We were nearing the burial chamber of Cleopatra!

Scaling a large pile of crumbled rock, we found another doorway at the base of the debris. It was almost completely blocked off. Only a small passage in the shape of a half moon remained open.

"Oh, jeez," Gannon said. "I don't know how much further I can go."

"You can do this, Gannon," I said. "Just take a deep breath and stay calm."

We slid down the rubble pile to the opening and shined our flashlights inside. Behind the doorway was a tunnel. It descended about fifteen feet and then leveled off.

"What do you think is down there?" Serene asked.

"Only one way to find out," I said.

"But if these rocks slide it could close off this opening and trap us inside the tunnel," Gannon said.

"That's a good point," Serene said. "We have to do something to make sure it doesn't get closed off. If we get trapped in there, we'll never get out."

"Let's see if we can fix some support around the opening," I said.

We found a large flat stone and with all of our might wedged it into the rubble pile, propping it over the opening to create a small protective barrier. It seemed sturdy enough to stop a rockslide. Or so we hoped.

Again, I took the lead. It was very hard to maneuver through the first part of the tunnel. The space was so tight we had to get down on our hands and knees and crawl. We've been in some hairy situations before. Several during this fellowship alone. But inching through this narrow shaft was easily one of the most uncomfortable situations of my life. The idea of getting buried by a rockslide made our anxiety even worse. There would be no getting out. Ever. At one point, I thought Gannon might lose it. We all stopped and I tried to calm him.

"Just try to relax, Gannon," I said, as calmly as I could.

"Sorry, but that's just not going to happen," he said, "so please just keep going so we can get the heck out of here."

Finally, the tunnel ended. I climbed out, stood upright. A wave of relief came over me. Serene came next, then Gannon, who was on the verge of hyperventilating.

"There better be another way out of here," he said, gasping. "Because there's no way I'm going back through there."

"Everyone follow me," I said, and took a step, but Serene reached out suddenly and pulled me back.

"Don't move," she said, and shined her flashlight along the ground.

Ahead of us was a dark void. If I had taken another step I would have gone hurling into an abyss. I moved my flashlight around and saw only darkness and empty space. We stood still, not wanting to make a wrong step, as the beams of our flashlights searched for a safe path that would lead us further into the tomb.

"Looks like there's some kind of bridge over there," Gannon said.

We shuffled along the ledge to the stone bridge, which was about as wide as a pillar, maybe two-feet tops. The bridge ran off further into the emptiness. On either side was more darkness.

"To cross this thing it's probably best if we slide one foot forward and then the other," I said. "That will make it easier to keep our balance."

I looked into the abyss.

"How far down do you think that goes?" Gannon asked.

"Let's not find out," Serene said.

I inched out onto the narrow bridge and started moving across. Serene followed. Gannon was last.

"Whatever is on the other side better be worth it, because this is totally insane," Gannon said.

"I have a feeling it will be," I said.

I checked to make sure the bridge was sturdy and then slid my right foot out, followed by my left. I was completely on the bridge. Shining the flashlight just ahead of me, I continued to cautiously make my way across.

"A hand railing would have been nice," Gannon said.

I almost laughed.

As I moved towards the middle, I noticed a sound, the low whoosh of wind, and felt a cool breeze coming from below.

Finally, I made it across and was back on solid ground. I took Serene's hand and helped her off the bridge. Gannon was close behind.

"Let's go," I said. "It can't be much further."

The air grew even cooler. The wind stronger. The whooshing sound louder. There was a flickering light up ahead.

As we rounded a limestone wall, an incredible phosphorescent waterfall came into view, illuminating the area with a fluorescent blue glow. Probably 20 feet across, it fell into a round area that had no bottom as far as we could see. Another abyss. We shined our lights up, searching for the waterfall's starting point, but found none. The water had no beginning and no end.

"This is the craziest thing I've ever seen," Gannon said.

"Where do you think all this water is coming from?" I asked Serene.

"We're very deep in the earth," she said. "It could be run-off from one of the massive aquifers that flows beneath the desert."

We kept on, moving behind the waterfall. A mist swirled around us. The rocks under our feet were slick. We moved slowly to keep from slipping. Narrow culverts ran along the walkway on either side of us, carrying a stream of glowing water. The walls of the tunnel flickered in blue light.

Following the illuminated path, we came to a grand entryway carved into the rock.

"Wow," Gannon said, his eyes wide with wonder. "Look at that!"

We slowly moved closer.

"Recognize this?" I asked, pointing to a stone overhead that was carved with hieroglyphics. It was the same inscription Dr. Aziz had translated earlier, but even if we hadn't noticed it, I could see that this was a tomb fit for the Queen of the Nile.

"Cleopatra!" Serene shouted. "This is it! This is her tomb!"

To the right of these hieroglyphics was another inscription. It read, "M·ANTONIVS·M·F·M·N."

"That's Latin!" Gannon shouted.

"Do you know what it says?" I asked.

"Well, I'm far from fluent," Gannon said, "but I remember the alphabet pretty well."

He studied the inscription for a moment.

"This is crazy," he said, "but I'm almost positive it says Mark Antony."

All at once, I was hit with an incredible rush of pride at being the first to find this tomb—a tomb that has escaped archeologists for centuries! At the same time, I felt awful that Dr. Aziz wasn't with us. This was his discovery, not ours. He had worked for over a decade in the hopes of one day enjoying this moment. He was far more deserving than we were. Be that as it may, events transpired as they did and there we were, entering the tomb of the world-famous Egyptian Queen, Cleopatra, and the legendary Roman General, Mark Antony.

"You're getting this all on video right?" I asked Gannon. "No one's going to believe it unless we have proof."

"Sorry, I'm so worried about being cursed, I almost forgot," Gannon said.

Gannon turned on his camera and started filming.

Framing the entryway to the tomb, two pillars of solid gold rose about fifteen feet into the air. Dimmed by thousands of years of dust, they were still spectacular. Each was etched with hieroglyphics and decorated in faded colors. When we stepped inside, what we found was almost incomprehensible. Channels of blue water ran beyond the pillars into the tomb, illuminating a treasure I couldn't have imagined in my wildest dreams. No disrespect to Howard Carter's discovery, but this made King Tut's treasure look like the collection of trinkets you might find in a little girl's jewelry box. And it was all displayed so neatly, like it had been placed by a museum curator.

There's an old saying, "you can't take it with you when you die." Well, the ancient Egyptians believed that you could. Inside the tomb were alabaster vases, elaborately decorated chairs with ivory and gold inlay, small painted boxes filled with gemstones, a magnificent wooden chariot with seats wrapped in leather, and numerous gilded statues carved into the likeness of animals—lions, jackals, and other unique creatures. There were also lots of other objects I couldn't identify, objects that would require further study of Egyptian art to describe accurately. In each of the four corners, life-sized, pharaoh-like figures stood guard.

"This is so beautiful!" Serene said.

We made our way through the tomb, doing a detailed examination of all the artifacts as we went. Serene and I made notes in our journals. Gannon continued taking video. Finally, we neared Cleopatra's sarcophagus. It lay flat on a slab of limestone against the far back wall of the tomb. Mark Antony's sarcophagus was to her right. There was a bust of each directly behind their coffin, which made them easy to identify. On either side of Cleopatra's bust was a golden asp, the snake she had chosen to initiate her journey into the afterlife.

Between the coffins sat a large chest, decorated with red and green stones and painted in colors that had somehow maintained their brightness over time. It, too, had Cleopatra's name inscribed on the top, along with other writing I couldn't translate. Given the chest's placement, perfectly centered between the two coffins, we gathered that it held significant importance.

"What do you think is inside?" Gannon asked.

"Only one way to find out," I said.

"I was afraid you'd say that."

Nerves shot through my arm as I reached out and put my hand atop the lid of the chest. Cautiously, I raised the lid and shined my flashlight inside. A sheet of yellowed linen was draped across the top. Gently, I lifted the corner of the sheet and pulled it back. Underneath were dozens of scrolls, tightly rolled, yellowed with age and bound by golden thread.

Serene gasped.

"The secret scrolls," she said.

"I can't believe it," I said. "It's all true."

Gannon moved in with his video camera.

The idea that the information contained in these scrolls explained many of ancient Egypt's greatest mysteries was almost unfathomable. The urge came over me to carefully pile the scrolls into our satchels. They looked to be in decent condition, but I couldn't be sure. As old as they were, I was afraid they might crumble in my hand if I moved them. It was too risky. If I made the wrong decision, all of the secrets contained within the scrolls could be lost. I dropped the linen cloth back over the top of the scrolls and closed the chest.

"Wow," I said. "I'm having a hard time catching my breath."

"This is all so unbelievable," Serene said. "I don't even know what to say."

"What do you think we should do with the scrolls?"

"I don't know. I wish Dr. Aziz was here."

"Me too. I'm afraid to touch them. We should probably leave them until he's with us."

Gannon kept his video camera rolling. He moved away from the chest and began capturing the detail along the top of Cleopatra's sarcophagus, which drew my attention away from the scrolls. Solid gold with red, blue, black, and white paint, the top of the coffin was sculpted in her likeness. Her face, shaped with delicate cheekbones and lips, seemed so lifelike, I felt like I was staring at the Queen herself. The eyes, especially. I would almost swear they could see me.

I held out my hand to brush away the dust that covered the coffin.

"Stop!" Gannon shouted. "I don't think you should touch it!"

As much as I wanted to dust them both off, slide open the

covers and see with my own eyes the mummies of Cleopatra and Mark Antony, two monumental figures in world history, I couldn't bring myself to do it.

"They should be left to rest in peace," Gannon said.

"I agree," Serene said.

I withdrew my hand.

"This is totally mind blowing and all," Gannon said, "but to be honest, I don't feel all that good about being here."

Gannon stepped to the sarcophagus.

"Cleopatra," he said, "please forgive us for disturbing your burial chamber. We mean no disrespect. Same goes for you, Mr. Antony. We're very sorry. Please accept our apology."

"That was nice, Gannon," I said, about to laugh. "You definitely scored some points for sincerity."

Gannon turned to us.

"I've got everything documented on camera," he said. "What do you say we get the heck out of here, like right now?"

"Good idea," Serene said.

"But what are we going to tell the tomb robbers?" I asked. "If we tell them what we've found, they'll blast their way in and steal everything."

We sat quietly for a moment, thinking of what to do. One thing was certain: We couldn't let them get their hands on the treasure. It's like Dr. Aziz told all of us, this is Egypt's heritage. And it was now our duty to protect it!

GANNON

Can't say I didn't warn everyone. Because I did. Over and over again. I mean, for real. Did anyone really think that we could just waltz on down to the center of the earth, intrude on the tomb of Cleopatra and Mark Antony, and not trigger some kind of crazy curse?

Please!

I know Wyatt and Serene took all kinds of detailed notes on what we found down there with the treasure and scrolls and all, so I'm just going to get right to what happened as a consequence, I believe, of disturbing their peace.

Okay, so, I'd just talked Wyatt out of being a bonehead and touching anything and was trying to hurry everyone up and get out of that tomb, when I detected a faint rumble. At first I thought I might turn around to see the mummies of Cleopatra and Mark Antony sliding the lids off their sarcophaguses or something, but it only took another second to realize what was really happening.

"Earthquake!" I screamed, and took off running for cover. The ground began to shake with such crazy force that my legs went out from under me and I landed flat on my stomach. The pillars in the chamber were wobbling back and forth. Large sections of stone crumbled to the ground all around me. Before I could even get back to my feet, a boulder crashed down right in front of my face, landing on top of my video camera, which was still strapped to my neck.

"I'm stuck!" I screamed.

Wyatt saw that I was struggling to free myself and quickly cut the camera strap with his knife. Serene helped lift me to my feet.

"My video camera got crushed!" I yelled.

"Better your camera than your head!" she shouted. "Now, let's get out of here!"

Just then, a wall of rubble came raining down from above, separating us from Cleopatra and Mark Antony.

"This way!" Serene yelled, and pulled me towards an opening in the far corner of the tomb. There, we ran into a tunnel and continued pushing forward. The ground was still shaking and the air was filled with all this dust and I lost sight of Wyatt and Serene. Rocks continued to fall all around and I closed my eyes, pretty much expecting to be crushed at any moment, pulverized by the crumbling earth, buried forever, just like Cleopatra and Mark!

When I opened my eyes, everything was still. The earth had stopped moving. A shaft of light came through the darkness. Dust was swirling everywhere and large rocks were piled all around me. Wyatt and Serene were nowhere to be seen.

I yelled their names.

There was no response. My heart was thumping and my leg hurt really bad. When I looked down, I found a large gash on the left calf muscle that was bleeding pretty good.

"Wyatt!" I yelled again. "Serene! Can you hear me?"

Oh, jeez, the thought of my brother and Serene being crushed under the rubble was making me sick. I stood and climbed over the boulders towards the light. My arms and legs were trembling.

I thought maybe I was losing too much blood from my leg and stopped long enough to grab my pocket knife, cut the sleeve off my shirt, and tie it tightly around the wound, hoping it would prevent me from bleeding to death.

"Wyatt! Serene!" I yelled again.

I heard a faint sound in the distance.

"Gannon," a voice said.

It was Serene.

"Help me."

"I'm coming, Serene!"

I climbed further towards the light and found her lying on her side. Her arm was pinned under a rock the size of a jeep tire.

"I'm trapped," she said.

"Can you still feel your arm?" I said, shining my flashlight into the area where her arm was stuck.

"Yes, I can."

That sure was good news.

"If I can roll the rock back, you should be able to get your arm out."

"Okay, but please be careful. There is a lot of pressure on it. I'm afraid any more will snap the bones."

I braced myself and pushed the rock with my hands,

but it didn't budge. So I stood over Serene and put my back against the rock, gripping it low and pulling the rock up with all my might. Surprisingly, the rock started to lift. Serene let out a scream and rolled away, holding her arm.

I dropped the rock and fell to her side thinking for sure that I had broken her arm.

"I'm so sorry, Serene! Are you okay?"

"I'm okay," she said, panting. "I pulled my arm free just in time. Thank you so much, Gannon."

Just then we heard a voice echo from above.

"If anyone's interested in some fresh air, I found an exit up here!"

I looked up and saw a silhouette of Wyatt's head surrounded on all sides by a bright white light. I couldn't have been happier. I mean, not only was he alive and uncrushed and all, he'd found a way out!

Serene and I climbed over a pile of rocks that led to the small hole. Once there, we grabbed Wyatt's hand and he helped pull us through the hole into the desert. Free from the tomb, we all fell onto our backs in the sand.

"That sure was a close call," Serene said.

"No kidding," I said, sitting up and looking around. There was no sign of anything in any direction. No camp, no city of Alexandria, just hills of sand.

"You know," I said, "I never thought I'd be so happy to be lost in the middle of the desert."

Wyatt sat up and looked around.

"This is not good," he said.

"Well, it's a heck of a lot better than being buried alive," I said.

"This is true."

"I'd like to take this opportunity to officially announce my retirement from archeology," I said. "From this point forward, I plan to focus exclusively on above-ground exploration."

The sun was hot and sweat beaded up on my forehead. My mouth was gritty with sand and bone dry.

"We need to get moving," Serene said. "We can't forget, the tomb robbers are still holding Dr. Aziz and the men at camp. They need our help."

Wyatt stood up and looked to the sky.

"It's mid-afternoon," he said, pointing at the sun. "This way is west, which makes this north. If we walk north we'll run into the Mediterranean. We should spot the camp along the way. How far away could it be?"

"But what're we going to do about the tomb robbers when we get there?" I asked. "Kindly ask them to pack up their machine guns and leave?"

"We'll figure it out as we walk," Serene said. "Let's get going."

The air was calm and the sky clear and it seemed to be getting hotter and hotter as we went. I was pretty much drenched with sweat and totally parched and my leg was throbbing where I had been cut. Sand was getting into my wound as I hobbled along through the desert, struggling just to keep up.

"If it gets this hot in the winter," I said, "I'd hate to see what it's like in the summer."

"If it were summer," Serene said, "we'd be dead already."

In places, a rare cloud would cast a shadow on the dunes that, if you didn't know better, looked like a pool of water. But we knew better, it was just a mirage. There was no water. And I'll say this, when you're lost in the desert, water is pretty much all you think about.

Another half-hour into our trek I was staggering and about to fall face down in the sand when an object appeared on the horizon, a small black dot moving slowly over the sandy hills.

"A Bedouin," Serene said.

"If we can get his attention he could save us," I said.

I immediately yanked off my shirt and began swinging it around like a helicopter propeller.

"Hey, Bedouin!" I yelled, running across the dune. "Help us! We need water or we're going to die!"

While I was doing all that screaming, I tripped and tumbled down the dune in a cloud of sand. That outburst pretty much used up the last of my energy, so I just stayed there staring at the blue sky, exhausted, unable to move, thinking that I had been cursed and was destined to die in the desert.

"That's one way to get his attention," Wyatt said, laughing, as he walked past me. "But I think I have a better idea."

He took off his explorer watch and used the stainless steel plate on the back to catch the sunlight and shoot a bright glare in the direction of the Bedouin.

Sure enough, it worked. I lifted my head and saw the black dot on the horizon turn and start moving in our direction, and thank goodness for that because if he'd ignored us, well, I wouldn't be writing this right now.

WYATT

A man in a long, flowing black robe and headdress came galloping up on a camel. He looked at us with piercing eyes and unwrapped the scarf from his mouth. When he spoke, his tone was harsh. I immediately worried that we had entered forbidden territory and would be punished.

Bedouins speak a different dialect of Arabic. Fortunately, Serene had spent time with a tribe the previous winter and understood the man. There was desperation in her voice as she spoke, and the man immediately softened to her.

He instructed his camel to sit and the man dismounted. From his satchel, he removed a goat-skinned canteen and handed it to Serene. She popped the plug from the top and poured water into her mouth. We all took turns drinking. The water was warm and not as clean as I would have liked, but we were dying of thirst, and when that's the case, hot murky water sure beats no water at all.

The Bedouin man took the canteen from us and put it back in his satchel. He spoke again and pointed to the camel.

Serene looked to us.

"Okay, let's go," she said.

It may seem impossible, and I will admit that it wasn't very comfortable, but all four of us climbed atop the camel and it stood up without a problem. We began at a steady pace through the desert. Not a trot or gallop, but a fast walk. The rhythmic roll of the camel's stride, the rocking back and forth, was almost soothing. Gannon tried to fight it, but within minutes he was slumped over, asleep.

Occasionally, Serene spoke to the Bedouin man. Mostly, though, we rode in silence. A little more than an hour into our journey, a tent village appeared on the horizon. Erected among a grove of palms with a dry riverbed running through it, the village seemed like a mirage.

"What are we doing?" I asked Serene.

"He wants to gather his men before we return to the excavation site," she explained. "Just in case there is any trouble with the tomb robbers."

"What is his name?" I asked, suddenly realizing that I had rudely forgotten to ask the name of this man who had saved us from the desert.

"Tahnoon," she said.

"Please thank Tahnoon for us."

Serene leaned in and spoke in his ear as we rode. He turned to us, smiled, and nodded.

GANNON

I love it when I wake up to find that I've already arrived at a destination and I have to say, the Bedouin camp sure was a sight for my tired, sore eyes. It was really primitive, but it was civilization. There were people and children all around dressed in desert robes and more camels than I could count, along with goats and chickens, water and food . . . life!

A young woman came up to us with a jug of water and handed each of us a little clay mug. It made me so happy I wrapped her in a big hug right then and there. It definitely caught her off guard, but she was a good sport and smiled and poured us a cup from the bucket. We guzzled it down like our lives depended on it, which, I guess they kind of did. This water was cool, clear, refreshing, and I could actually feel it sliding down my throat and into my stomach.

"May I have another cup?" I asked, pointing to the water.

The woman nodded and poured me another glass and I drank it down just as fast and asked for another. I didn't think there was enough water in the ocean to quench my thirst, but we all managed to drink until we were full and afterwards found a spot of shade under a palm tree where we fell into the sand for a rest. Another woman appeared with a tray of flat bread and hummus and a pile of dates.

We'd worked up a pretty serious appetite in the desert and went about scarfing down that food like a bunch of hungry jackals. After, Serene found someone to help me clean and bandage my leg. The Bedouin people sure did take good care of us and I couldn't be more grateful.

While we rested in the shade, Tahnoon went through the camp rounding up every able man. Some boys no older than us prepared camels. I mean, that they would do this, help us in this way, maybe even risking their own lives for people they had just met, was totally incredible.

Tahnoon came back and lifted his arm, yelling something to his people. When he was finished, we all raised our arms in the air, too, and shouted before climbing atop our camels. Some carried rifles over their shoulders and others had swords strapped to their hips, which brought back an empty, sick feeling to my stomach.

Sitting on top of Tahnoon's camel, I noticed that my hands were shaking. I was seriously worried that some of these brave Bedouin people might die unnecessarily. I mean, it was impossible to guess what the tomb robbers might do when we arrived at camp, but it wasn't much of a stretch to assume that they would simply open fire. I was scared that I would never see my parents again and pretty much the only thing that kept me from freaking out was witnessing the bravery of the Bedouins. In them I found strength.

A warm and steady wind blew sand through the air, stinging the side of my face. I turned my head away from the wind as we marched back into the desert, a Bedouin Army one hundred strong at our side.

WYATT

Tahnoon, our Bedouin friend, had saved us from the desert, but before we had time to appreciate our good fortune, we were approaching camp, likely to face the most dangerous situation yet.

Tahnoon split the Bedouins into two groups, sending one around to the opposite dune. There were approximately fifty people in each group. The idea was to come into camp from both sides and form a circle, cutting off all exits.

When the second group was in place, we began our march up the dune. As we approached the top, the camp and excavation site came into view. Men scurried all over. Gannon pointed out the tomb robbers to Tahnoon and he passed along the information to his men. They were easy to spot in their uniforms. We counted twelve in total.

On the opposite side of the camp, the second unit rose up along the crest of a far dune. What a sight it was! Camel-backed Bedouins in perfect formation, their long black robes blowing in the wind like phantoms of the desert, the rightful protectors of this spectacular land.

It didn't take long for us to be noticed. A gunshot was fired into the air from camp. Tahnoon removed a rifle from his satchel and returned fire, a single shot into the air, warning the tomb robbers that we were armed, as well. I looked at Gannon who was wiggling his fingers around in his ears, and would have laughed if I wasn't so afraid.

Then Tahnoon gave the signal. Raising his arm he shouted something that could have only meant "charge!" We lurched forward. I was riding with one of Tahnoon's cousins, a man named Zayed, and took hold of the saddle rope to keep from falling off as the camel came down the dune.

Several shots were fired, some from the Bedouins, others from a distance. More warning shots, I hoped, but couldn't be sure. Everyone in camp ran around frantically in different directions. A group of tomb robbers made a break for it, trying to charge up the dune before the camp was completely closed off, but their escape was blocked by several Bedouins with rifles drawn. The men surrendered immediately, throwing their weapons into the sand.

But there was more gunfire in camp. Zayed even fired a shot into the air and made a sudden sharp turn, throwing me off the back of the camel. I landed hard on the ground, knocking the wind out of myself. The thunderous sound of hooves pounding into the sand rumbled around me on all sides. Sand was kicked into my eyes. I couldn't see.

More shots were fired. Bullets whizzed through the air. I rolled over, covered my head, thinking for sure I was about to be trampled. Suddenly, someone was on top of me. They grabbed me under the arms and began dragging me away. I pushed with my legs to help this person who was attempting to pull me to safety. We made our way through the chaos and into a tent. The person dragging me fell onto the ground next to me, gasping for breath. It was James.

"We all thought you were dead, mate!" he said. "Buried in the tomb forever!"

"We almost were," I said, spitting sand from my mouth. "I'm glad to see you're okay, too."

"After the earthquake it's been so chaotic, the tomb robbers forgot all about me."

We stood and caught our breath.

"I'm curious, mate. How in the world did you coordinate this Bedouin raid?"

"I'll tell you later," I said, "We have to get back out there."

James and I moved to the door of the tent.

Things outside had settled. It seemed the battle was over. Then, near the entrance of the tomb, I spotted two men. Their guns were drawn on each other. A second later, I realized it was Tahnoon and the commander. He appeared to be the only tomb robber that had not surrendered.

Dr. Aziz and Khalid stood off to the side. Gannon and Serene were behind them. I was relieved to see that they were all okay, but very afraid for Tahnoon. Judging by what I knew of the commander, he wasn't going to give up without a fight. They both yelled at one another, their fingers on the triggers of their rifles. Two other Bedouins had their guns drawn on the commander. He was not going to get away, that was for sure. I just hoped he realized that before someone got shot.

Dr. Aziz wasn't about to sit back and see how this would play out. He took the matter into his own hands, literally. In one fluid motion, he lifted his arm and threw a rock at the commander. Like a fastball from a major league pitcher, his aim was dead on, hitting the commander hard on the side of his head. The commander grunted and dropped to his knees. He was immediately tackled and dragged away by several men, still groggy after that thump to the skull.

"What a shot!" Khalid said. "I didn't know you had it in you!"

"Nice throw, Doc," Gannon said. "If archeology hadn't been your passion, I bet you could have played for the Yankees."

"I got lucky," he said, chuckling. "Never touched a baseball in my life. Growing up, soccer was my sport."

The tomb robbers had all been detained and were being escorted to the police station in Alexandria. My guess is that their days of tomb robbing are over.

Dr. Aziz gathered us in his tent. It was myself, Gannon, Serene, James and Tahnoon. One by one he approached us, kissing us on the cheek and giving us a firm hug. There were tears in his eyes when he spoke.

"First, I want to say thank you," he said. "What you've done on this expedition was above and beyond the call of duty. Your actions saved our lives."

"It was Tahnoon and his people," Gannon said, gesturing to him. "They deserve all the credit."

Serene translated what Gannon had said.

Tahnoon bowed.

Dr. Aziz spoke to Tahnoon in Arabic.

Serene translated it back to English for us, "Dr. Aziz said that the Bedouins are a proud and brave people and that we will forever be indebted."

Again, Tahnoon bowed.

"Now," Dr. Aziz said, turning to us with wonder in his eyes, "how on earth did you get out of there? The entrance was completely closed off by the earthquake. Is there another way into the tomb? Since you are standing here, I assume there must be!"

"You know," Gannon said, "we're not really sure. After the earthquake, we climbed out of a small hole and found ourselves somewhere in the middle of the desert."

"The distance we traveled underground didn't equate to the long distance we had to travel to get back to camp," I said. "Honestly, I don't understand it."

"That is very interesting," Dr. Aziz said. "Another Egyptian mystery, I suppose."

"What about the tomb itself?" Khalid said.

"Yes, we must know." Dr. Aziz continued. "What did you find? What is down there? The chambers can no longer be seen on the radar. It's as if everything underground has disappeared."

"I'm sorry to have to tell you this," I said, "but I think the entire complex was buried in rubble."

"Please, describe the complex to me! Describe the tomb! Was Cleopatra inside? Was Mark Antony at her side? I must know!"

Dr. Aziz was shaking with excitement as we all described what we had seen.

"Did you document any of this?" he asked.

Serene and I showed him the notes we'd made in our journals.

"That's all we have," I said. "Gannon's camera was destroyed during the earthquake."

He took the journals in his hand and sat quietly for a moment, gathering his thoughts.

"Your journals have a value beyond measure," Dr. Aziz finally said. "With your permission, I will keep copies of your field notes at the Youth Exploration Society offices in Cairo."

"Of course," I said.

"It would be an honor," Serene replied.

"It could be the only record we'll ever have of Cleopatra's tomb," Dr. Aziz continued.

"What do you mean?" Gannon asked. "We know she's here."

"Yes, but the damage from the earthquake was so severe, it may be that we're never able to find the tomb again."

"I'm really sorry we couldn't help you discover your 100th tomb," Gannon said. "But I said it before, and I'll say it again. Maybe some things aren't meant to be found. They're meant to remain a secret. Forever."

Dr. Aziz nodded.

"You might be right, Gannon," he said. "You might be right."

GANNON

When we got back to our hotel in Cairo the international press was waiting. Somehow word had gotten out and people were desperate to find out if all the rumors were true. It was a total madhouse, with flashbulbs going off in our faces and people shouting all kinds of questions.

"Tell us what you saw inside the tomb!"

"Did you really find Cleopatra?"

"Was Mark Antony buried with her?"

"What is the location of the tomb?"

"Do you have photographs?"

"How much damage was done by the earthquake?"

Dr. Aziz told us he would put out an official statement in the coming days explaining everything that had happened, so until then we're keeping our mouths shut.

My parents muscled their way into the frenzy and helped pull us through the masses into the hotel lobby. We ran past the front desk and escaped into the elevator, while a few security guards did their best to hold back the press. Once the doors of the elevator closed, it was really quiet all of a sudden. We all just looked at each other in silence while soothing elevator music played from the speakers.

Finally, my mom spoke.

"You mind explaining what's going on?" she asked.

"Seems you boys are quite the media sensation," my dad added. "Can't wait to hear what you got yourselves into this time."

"I don't have the energy to explain it all right now," I said. "I'm as tired as a camel who just crossed the Sahara. Besides, you wouldn't believe us anyway. Trust me on that one."

"Of course we would," my mom said. "Come on. Tell us everything that happened."

"You're just going to have to read our journals."

I took my journal from my pack and handed it to my mom. When she flipped it open, sand poured onto the floor. The pages were dirty and brittle from exposure to the dry, desert air. Sloppy handwriting filled each page from top to bottom.

"This thing is filthy," she said. "As far as your grade is concerned, I wouldn't keep my hopes up. For starters, the penmanship is awful."

"Oh, come on, Mom. If you shoveled dirt from sunrise to sunset, your penmanship wouldn't look so hot either. We could barely lift our pens at the end of the day."

"I'll tell you something else," Wyatt added. "I expect a top grade and nothing less. If you only knew what we went through, you'd be amazed we wrote a single page."

"Okay, relax," Mom said, "When I grade your work, I'll take that all into consideration."

The elevator door opened, and we walked to our room.

"I'm really intrigued," my dad said, taking the journal from my mom. "I'm going to start reading right away."

My dad opened the door and we entered the room.

"Whatever you do," I said, "don't wake me. I don't know about Wyatt, but I could sleep for a week straight."

"Without a doubt," Wyatt agreed.

"Enjoy the adventure," I said to my parents, and collapsed onto the bed.

I was out before my head hit the pillow.

A view of Cairo and the Nile

WYATT

We had one last thing to do before we left Egypt.

This morning the hotel manager arranged for a car to pick us up a block away. He led us to an exit in the back corner of the hotel, as the press was still camped out in the lobby. From there, we sprinted across the street and jumped into the car.

"Khan al-Khalili bazaar, please," Gannon said.

We found the shopkeeper seated at a table in the corner of his store, sipping a cup of coffee. Oddly enough, he did not look surprised to see us.

"The famous young archeologists," he said. "I've heard the news. So, tell me. Is it true?"

Gannon smiled and nodded.

"We came to tell you that your grandfather's artifact played a major role in our discovery," Gannon said. "We were about to call off the excavation, when I found another tile just like it. That gave us the confidence to continue the dig. Before we left Egypt, we wanted to return it to you."

Gannon held out the tile.

The shopkeeper took it in his hands.

"I knew it was true," he said. "My grandfather was close."

"Very close," I said.

Knowing this with certainty seemed to give the shop-keeper peace of mind. His grandfather was, in fact, a great archeologist, and very nearly made one of the greatest discoveries of all time.

"And I owe you an apology," I said.

"What for?" the shopkeeper asked.

"For doubting you," I said. "I'm sorry, but I thought you were trying to scam us."

The shopkeeper laughed.

"I understand," the man said. "There are a few shopkeepers in this market who would do just that."

"It's like they say back home," Gannon said, "a few bad apples can spoil the bunch."

The shopkeeper looked at the piece again. A smile came over his face. He then gripped it tightly in his hand, turned to us and made a slight bow.

"May your journey lead you to a better understanding of those things which are truly important in life," he said.

"If you don't mind me asking," Gannon said, "what would those things be?"

His smile grew wider.

"That's for you to discover."

GANNON

MARCH 21
CAIRO

Touring the Great Pyramids of Giza

We're flying back to Colorado tonight and I've just finished packing, which basically involved stuffing a bunch of dirty clothes into my backpack. There's still about an hour before we leave, so I took a seat on our balcony and have been looking out over the city with the Great Pyramids in the distance. Thinking of all the amazing stuff we learned, one thing in particular keeps coming to mind. Even though our mission wasn't a total success and we weren't able to unveil Cleopatra and Mark Antony's tomb to the world and get our names printed in the history books and all that cool stuff, we were still able to prove what Dr. Aziz kept telling us throughout the fellowship: When you're pursing your goals, it pays to be persistent. Don't give up when the going gets tough, and it is definitely going to get tough. That's a guarantee. And when it does, you have to be strong, believe in yourself, and keep going. Really, that's the thing I hope to take away from this whole experience.

Okay, now. In closing, I think a special thanks is in order. To all you ancient Egyptians dwelling in the afterlife who, in some mystical way, played a part in deciding that it wasn't yet my time to join you, much obliged.

Ma`a as-salaamah, Egypt.

GANNON & WYATT's

TRAVEL MAP

Siberia

St. Petersburg, Russia

Moscow, Russia

Gobi Desert, Mongolia

The Great Wall of China

Himalayas, Nepal

Masada, Israel

Ruins of Petra, Jordan

Persian Gulf

Cairo, Egypt

Tibet

Taj Mahal, India

Varanasi, India

Hong Kong, China

Angkor Wat, Cambodia

The Serengeti

Kho Phi Phi, Thailand

Equator

Nairobi

Ngorongoro Crater

Okavango Delta

Bali

Darwin

Fiji

Mauritius Islands

The Great Barrier Reef

Kalahari Desert

Australian Outback

Cape of Good Hope

Mt. Cook, New Zealand

Antarctica

McMurdo Station

AUTHORS' NOTE

At the time of writing this authors' note, the nation of Egypt is in a state of unrest. The country's current situation is much too complex to analyze from afar. However, what is clear to everyone who follows the news is that the good people of Egypt are suffering. Amidst political turmoil and violence, many Egyptians struggle to provide for their families; their jobs, their safety, and their general welfare are in jeopardy.

Egypt was home to one of history's greatest civilizations, and much of the country's spectacular antiquities remain unspoiled. To tour Egypt today is to marvel at the potential of human achievement. For these reasons, Egypt is a very popular travel destination. Many of us have wondered what it would be like to see the relics of ancient Egypt with our own eyes—to descend into the tomb of Tutankhamen, to walk among the ornate pillars of Karnak's Great Hypostyle Hall, to reach out and touch one of the massive stone blocks at the base of the Great Pyramid.

Tourism is a critical component of the Egyptian economy. In recent years, however, vacationers have been foregoing trips to Egypt, citing fear for their safety as the primary reason. Such concerns are valid given the current instability. In time, though, a visit to Egypt will once again prove enticing, for at its roots Egypt is a magnificent place.

During our trip, we experienced Egyptian kindness and hospitality firsthand. People would frequently stop us and ask, "Where are you from?" When we told them that we were from the United States, the response was always friendly. "How are you enjoying Egypt?" was the question most people asked next. In Luxor, a family even invited us into their home for dinner. These gracious hosts opened their door to strangers—foreigners no less.

The Egyptian children, like all young people, are playful and innocent. Interacting with the youth is a clear reminder of why we can be hopeful for the future. Inherently children are open-minded, pure in thought, and compassionate toward others. It is our responsibility to strengthen these virtues in our children, instilling in them a lifelong tolerance and understanding of other people and cultures. To quote John F. Kennedy, "For, in the final analysis, our most basic common link is that we all inhabit this small planet. We all breathe the same air. We all cherish our children's future. And we are all mortal."

To our friends in Egypt, we send our best wishes. May your future be blessed with opportunity, peace, and happiness.

Gannon and Wyatt in Giza

MEET THE "REAL-LIFE"
GANNON AND WYATT

Have you ever imagined traveling the world over? Fifteen-year-old twin brothers Gannon and Wyatt have done just that. With a flight attendant for a mom and an international businessman for a dad, the spirit of adventure has been nurtured in them since they were very young. When they got older, the globe-trotting brothers had an idea—why not share with other kids all of the amazing things they've learned during their travels? The result is the book series, Travels with Gannon and Wyatt, a video web series, blog, photographs from all over the world, and much more. Furthering their mission, the brothers also cofounded the Youth Exploration Society (Y.E.S.), an organization of young people who are passionate about making the world a better place. Each Travels with Gannon & Wyatt book is loosely based on real-life travels. Gannon and Wyatt have actually been to Botswana and tracked rhinos on foot. They have traveled to the Great Bear Rainforest in search of the mythical spirit bear, and explored the ancient tombs of Egypt. During these "research missions," the authors, along with Gannon and Wyatt, often sit around the campfire collaborating on an adventure tale that sets two young explorers on a quest for the kind of knowledge you can't get from a textbook. We hope you enjoy the novels that were inspired by these fireside chats. As Gannon and Wyatt like to say, "The world is our classroom, and we're bringing you along."

HAPPY TRAVELS!

Want to become a member of the
Youth Exploration Society
just like Gannon and Wyatt?

Check out our website. That's where you'll learn how to
become a member of the Youth Exploration Society, an organization of young people, like yourself, who love to travel and
are interested in world geography, cultures, and wildlife.

The website also includes:

Information about Egypt, amazing photos of the pyramids,
and complete episodes of our award-winning web series shot
on location with Gannon and Wyatt!

BE SURE TO CHECK IT OUT!

WWW.YOUTHEXPLORATIONSOCIETY.ORG

ACKNOWLEDGMENTS

Guiding us on our epic Egyptian adventure were many wonderful people to whom we owe a great debt of gratitude. We would like to thank the Emmy Award-winning producer, Leslie Grief, and the awesome crew of *Chasing Mummies*; the world-famous archeologist, Dr. Zahi Hawass, for allowing special access to some of Egypt's most spectacular tombs; film and television producer, Mohammed Gohar, our dependable producer, Bibo, and the exceptional crew at Video Cairo Sat; Homdi and his family for inviting us into their home; and the kind and hospitable people of Egypt who often went out of their way to assure we had a first-rate experience. Also, a special thanks to producer and cinematographer Robert Smyth for lending his talents to our first major production. And last, but not least, to our favorite explorers, Gannon and Wyatt, for climbing into dark tombs and tight spaces where most people would never go.

ABOUT THE AUTHORS

PATTI WHEELER, producer of the web series Travels with Gannon & Wyatt: Off the Beaten Path, began traveling at a young age and has nurtured the spirit of adventure in her family ever since. For years it has been her goal to create children's books that instill the spirit of adventure in young people. The Youth Exploration Society and Travels with Gannon & Wyatt are the realization of her dream.

KEITH HEMSTREET is a writer, producer, and cofounder of the Youth Exploration Society. He attended Florida State University and completed his graduate studies at Appalachian State University. He lives in Aspen, Colorado, with his wife and three daughters.

Make sure to check out the first two books in our award-winning series:

Botswana

Great Bear Rainforest

Look for upcoming books and video from these and other exciting locations:

Greenland

Iceland

Tanzania

Ireland

The American West

If you enjoyed Gannon and Wyatt's adventure in
Egypt, make sure to read the book that started it all . . .

TRAVELS WITH **GANNON & WYATT**

BOTSWANA

Nautilus Award Silver Medal Winner
Winner of Five Purple Dragonfly Book Awards
Moonbeam Children's Book Award Silver Medalist
Colorado Book Award Finalist

"Botswana has rarely had a portrayal that so accurately captures the physical and emotional spirit of Africa . . . This is a brilliant first of what I hope will be many books in a travel-novel series."

—*Sacramento Book Review*

Discover more adventures in . . .

TRAVELS WITH **GANNON & WYATT**

GREAT BEAR
RAINFOREST

"A groundbreaking series of adventurous stories like nothing else in children's literature. Kids of all ages and from all backgrounds love these stories because they are packed with action, humor, mystery, and fun adventures."

—Mark Zeiler, middle school language arts teacher, Orlando, Florida

MY JOURNAL NOTES

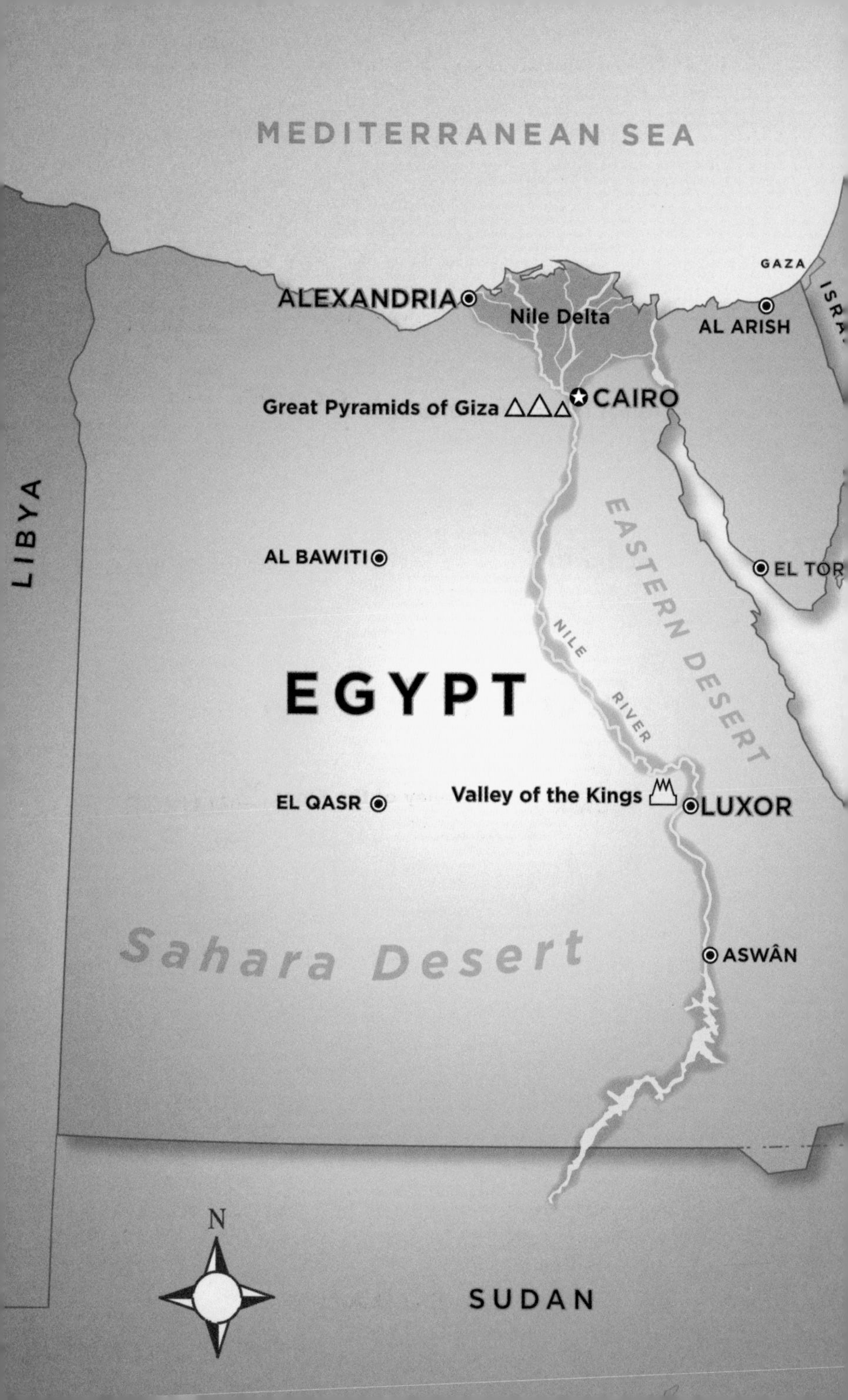

MEDITERRANEAN SEA

GAZA

ALEXANDRIA ◉

Nile Delta

AL ARISH ◉

ISRA

Great Pyramids of Giza △△△ ★ **CAIRO**

LIBYA

AL BAWITI ◉

◉ **EL TOR**

NILE

RIVER

EGYPT

EASTERN DESERT

EL QASR ◉

Valley of the Kings ⛰ ◉ **LUXOR**

Sahara Desert

◉ **ASWÂN**

N

SUDAN